B
SC OOL
RUMOURS

BOOK THREE IN THE
AMBERWOOD HALL SERIES

ELEANOR DIXON

Burreau Publishing

Published by Burreau Publishing 2022

Gorsky Road, Shropshire TF9 2JD

Print Book ISBN 978-1-8382708-4-1

Front Cover design and illustration: Rob Bennet

Contents

I dedicate this book to you, my reader!
Because without you, there would be no books. And if you are reading this, you are very special to me.
Carry on reading!

Chapter One

Lauren glanced up as the first flake of artificial snow floated down to the stage. She just had time to glimpse Rodney, the ghost of Amberwood Hall's stable boy, grinning as he waved his arms to make the snow swirl and eddy.

The music swelled and Lauren felt like she would take off and fly as the dancers leaped through snowflakes that were turning into a blizzard thanks to Rodney's antics. The cheeky ghost was only visible to Lauren, and she tried not to laugh as he flew round and round the stage whipping up the snowstorm.

She needed to concentrate! The finale to the Christmas show was already a frenzy of fast moves and changing places. She didn't have time to watch Rodney.

As the music soared to a crescendo, Lauren stepped onto the pointe of her right foot and pirouetted into position in front of Luis Nguyen, a senior boy. Mirroring her at the other side of the stage, her best friend Katie took her pose in front of another senior, Zachary Flores.

Lauren tightened her core and lifted her weight out of her hips as Luis placed his hands around her waist. A quick check told her she and Katie were synchronised. Then, on the last chord of the music, the boys swooped Lauren and Katie onto their shoulders as though they weighed no more than dolls. Lauren lodged the side of her foot against Luis's chest for added balance while his left arm circled her waist and kept her safe. His right arm followed the same circle as hers and they finished with a flourish in an open arabesque position with Lauren's arm high, Luis's low. Lauren looked towards Katie, whose smile matched her own.

The applause thundered through the auditorium and Lauren thought her heart would burst with happiness. What a wonderful way to end the term! She wished this moment could last forever. She stole a look into the wings where Grace, Amberwood's principal resident ghost, was clasping her hands to her chest in an expression of sheer delight. Grace had helped Lauren in her first year at Amberwood and, along with Katie, was Lauren's other best friend.

All too soon, the curtain cut them off from the audience, and Luis and Zachary lowered the girls to the ground. "Well done, kid!" Luis grinned and gave Lauren a high five before sauntering off stage with the rest of his year.

Lauren drew in her breath and gazed round. She didn't want to leave the stage yet. She wanted to savour this moment: the smell of the resin from the ballet shoes, the sound of applause dying away, the disembodied swell of conversation from the audience behind the heavy velvet curtains, the shuffle of the dancers' feet as they made their way to the wings and the dressing rooms. She ran to the heavy curtains and made a tiny gap so that she could peer through to the auditorium.

There was Mum and her new boyfriend Nick. They seemed to be getting on well with Jay's parents. Then Lauren's view was blocked as the huge shape of Hunter Jenson, a famous black rapper from New York, rose out of a seat a few rows in front. He was a friend of Ethan's dad and, as he was on tour in England, had come to the show in place of Ethan's parents, who couldn't get there from New York where they lived. Jenson's gold jewellery glinted in the house lights, and Lauren could almost see the entire audience reflected in his huge dark glasses. He'd caused quite a sensation by his appearance and Ethan had been delighted. He hadn't been expecting anyone to come to see him in the show.

Lauren let the curtains fall back into place. Turning back to the stage, she blew a stray snowflake off her nose. Excited chatter filled the air as the Year Nines swapped notes on what had gone right or wrong for them in the show. Then Lauren heard someone call her name. She swivelled round to see Jay limping onto the stage with his walking stick in one hand, a camera in the other. His leg was healing well but he'd be off dancing for a few more weeks. His face was one huge grin.

"That was awesome," Jay said. "The atmosphere was electric! How on earth did they get the snow to swirl around like that? You can't believe how good it looked from the front. I wish I could have taken part!"

"Well, that'll teach you to fall off roofs," Lauren teased her friend and classmate. "I'm sure you'll be fine by the time we do another show. Did you get any of it on your phone?"

Katie and Ethan came over as she was speaking. Their fingers kept brushing together till Ethan took hold of Katie's hand properly. So they were officially dating, Lauren thought with a fuzzy feeling in her stomach. That would make Katie's Christmas!

"Better than that," Jay said, indicating the camera. "Mark's dad brought this and let me do the filming so that he could relax and watch the show."

"Heads!" came a warning yell from the grid above, and Lauren and friends jumped and made a mad dash for the wings. Lauren looked back as ropes uncoiled and dangled mere feet from where they had just been standing. She sighed with delight. Even if she worked, slept and ate on stage, she didn't feel she would ever get enough of it.

"Time to go!" called a Year Ten stagehand, waving a broom at the group of friends. "We need to strike the scenery and you're in the way!" He began to sweep up the artificial snow. The sound of hammers working on supports and scenery flats made it difficult to talk anyway, so the group of friends drifted away to join their classmates who were collecting their belongings from backstage.

Mark, the fourth boy in Year Nine whose dad had lent Jay the camera, joined them. "Let's have a look!" he said, holding out his hand.

Jay handed the camera to him. "You'd have done a better job probably," he conceded, "the way you're always messing with cameras and computers, but I did my best."

Everyone clamoured round to see the footage. Before long, most of Year Nine were crushing up, standing on pointe, or pushing on each other's shoulders to get a better view of the tiny screen.

"I knew I'd missed that beat," Emily groaned. "You look amazing, though, Alli!"

"Well, get out of the way and let me see!" Allison snapped.

Mark held the camera above his head. "I'll WhatsApp you all the video," he said. "Then you can look at it on your own screens, full size."

"Good idea," agreed Lauren, who felt like she was suffocating with so many hot, sweaty bodies pressing around her. "Time we weren't here, anyway. Our parents will be waiting to take us home."

"Not mine," Jay said, falling into step beside her as they made their way out of the stage door and skirted the auditorium, heading for the main house. "It's too far to drive now. They've booked a room in town for the night and we're leaving tomorrow morning."

"Doesn't look like we'll be leaving soon either," Katie chuckled, and she pointed back towards the glass-walled foyer. Everyone turned to see Katie's film star mum, surrounded by a large group of students clutching pieces of paper and pens. "This always happens!"

At that moment, Mrs Herriott appeared behind Mrs Dansfield. The sight of the students' faces turning scarlet, and the speed with which they melted away, made it unnecessary to hear what the headmistress was saying. Katie's mum smiled gratefully at Mrs Herriott, and Katie sighed. "Looks like we'll be heading off soon after all. Merry Christmas, everyone!"

"I need to run!" Ethan was staring at his mobile. "Dad's friend didn't just come to watch the show. He's coming home to New York with me. And we're going to the airport NOW. Bye, everyone! See you next term!" He sped away towards the boys' dormitories in the stable block to change.

"Are you coming?" Lauren tilted her head towards Katie.

"I'll see you in the dorm," Katie said quickly. "I just want to say goodbye to Ethan." And she ran after him calling, "Ethan, wait!"

"Imagine flying all the way to New York with someone as famous as Hunter Jenson," Jay said.

"Or someone as big!" Lauren quipped. "I hope they're going premium or whatever it's called. That rapper guy will take up two seats just with his gold jewellery." She shivered. "Sorry, Jay, but I'm going to split. It's freezing out here."

"See you before you go?" Jay called.

Lauren waved her hand and darted into the house and upstairs to the dormitory. It didn't take her long to change and shove the last-minute things into her case. Most of her stuff was staying at school and she only had one case and her rucksack.

She called goodbye to her dormitory mates and began dragging her bags along the corridor.

"Lauren!" Matron's voice stopped her at the top of the stairs. "I was just about to send someone to find you." She handed Lauren a piece of paper. "This is the new girl's email address. I'm counting on you to get in touch and make friends. Then you can look after her when she arrives next term."

Lauren took the paper and read the name. Nyree Peterson. She frowned. "Why does she need looking after? Everyone will show her the ropes and make her feel welcome."

Matron looked like she could say something on that subject, but wouldn't. Instead, she put her hand on Lauren's shoulder and gave it a quick squeeze. "Nyree is very young, Lauren," she explained. "She will be in Year Nine with you, but she's only eleven years old. She's extremely bright, apparently, and will have to do some lessons on her own. For instance, maths! She's even way ahead of the Year Elevens."

Lauren's jaw dropped. "Wow. That might be handy! She can help me!" she joked.

Matron looked at her sternly. "I want her to feel that she already has a friend before she gets here," she continued. "It's all going to be strange for her, especially coming from South Africa. Remember, she's leaving home for the first time, and she won't get to see her parents again till Easter."

Lauren nodded. "I'll do my best, Matron."

"I know you will. Now, have a lovely holiday and I'll see you next term!"

Matron turned back the way she had come, and Lauren continued down the stairs. Suddenly she felt a rush of cold air. She stopped in the middle of the staircase and looked round.

A shimmer of transparent cornflower blue swirled and solidified until, standing before her, was Grace.

"And just where did you think you were going?" Grace scolded. "How could you even think of leaving for the holidays without saying goodbye? I've been trying to talk to you since the end of the show, but you've been surrounded by people constantly."

"I wasn't going to leave," Lauren protested. "I was just taking my stuff down, then I was coming to find you. And Rodney. Honest!"

Grace smoothed her frown. "I don't know where Rodney's got to," she said. "And anyway, he's not allowed up here by the girls' dormitories. He's probably haunting the stable block. Giving the boys something to think about before they go!"

"It would be useful if he was here." Lauren resumed bumping her case down the stairs. "At least he can move stuff. He could give me a bit of help with this!"

Grace floated beside her. "I'm going to miss you," she said. "But you'll have a lovely Christmas. And your mum's friend looks so kind."

Lauren pressed her lips together and avoided Grace's eyes. "Well, we'll see," she muttered. She was still holding out on her decision about Nick. He seemed okay. But she wasn't sure she wanted things to change at home. She'd only just got used to her mum being on her own, even though it was nearly two years since Dad died.

Giving herself a mental shake, she looked back at Grace. "Wish I could give you a big hug!"

"Me too!" smiled Grace. "Merry Christmas, Lauren. See you next term!"

Chapter Two

On Christmas morning, Lauren woke with a fluttery feeling of excitement in her stomach. She couldn't wait to see her brother Liam's face when he opened the present she had bought him. And she just knew that Mum would adore the pale pink jumper Lauren had found on the last weekend of term.

She sat up and shone her torch on the bottom of the bed. Yes! There, as every year, was her Christmas stocking. Quietly, so as not to wake Liam, who was sleeping just the other side of a thin plasterboard dividing their room, she pulled the goodies out of the stocking.

Apart from the inevitable tangerine and walnuts, a family tradition from when her mum was a child, Lauren pulled the wrapping off a pair of earmuffs, a card with six different pairs of earrings, a new hairbrush, some miniature bottles of perfume and some heart-shaped scented candles. Then, tucked right at the bottom, were two pairs of socks! Lauren hugged them to her cheek. She had a thing about pulling on a new pair of socks. She just loved that feeling!

Munching on her tangerine, she sent a text to Katie. "You awake?" She waited for a few minutes, but there was no reply. Nothing from Nyree either, though that wasn't a surprise. Lauren had emailed her to introduce herself, as Matron had asked, and then suggested that they text instead of email because Lauren didn't want to have to keep asking Liam to use his computer. But Nyree wasn't very chatty and had sent only one or two texts in reply to Lauren's daily messages.

Lauren slipped out of bed and into her fleece dressing gown. She would make Mum a cup of tea and take it to her in bed.

But when Lauren went to the top of the stairs, she could see the kitchen light was on. Samantha Mason was already up. Lauren bounded down and into the kitchen.

"Happy Christmas!" she shouted as she threw her arms round her mum's waist in a big bear hug.

"Happy Christmas, my love," Mum replied, hugging her in return and kissing the top of her head. "Is that lazy brother of yours awake?"

Lauren shook her head and poured some cereal into a bowl that was already on the table. "'Course not," she said, reaching for the milk. "I'm starving! Can I have toast as well?"

Mum waved her hand towards the toaster. "It's already on. But it would be nice to have breakfast all together. Go and wake Liam."

Lauren grimaced. "I was rather hoping to keep my head safely on my shoulders today," she muttered, but she went back upstairs and gently shook her sleeping brother.

"Gerroff," Liam growled as he turned his back on her and continued to doze.

"It's Christmas," Lauren whispered, and she tickled his ear with a bookmark she found lying on the bedside table. "And me and Mum want to open prezzies. Get up!"

Liam mumbled and turned onto his back. Lauren snapped on the bedside light and Liam's hand flew to his eyes. "Must you?" he groaned.

"Yep! Anything to get you up! Come on, Liam. Just for today!" She grabbed his stocking from the foot of the bed and dangled it in his face. "Look! Father Christmas has been!"

Liam snatched it off her and yawned. Then he dragged himself into a sitting position and started to shake the small gifts onto the duvet.

"Peel that for me," he demanded, throwing the tangerine at Lauren. "It'll help me wake up."

Lauren obliged, then went to the door. "I'll see you downstairs. Hurry, or you won't get any breakfast."

An hour later, Lauren, Liam, and Mum were sitting around the Christmas tree in their tiny living room. A pile of discarded wrapping filled the space on the floor around Lauren where she was sitting in turn-out position. Her eyes were glued on Liam, who was opening her present to him.

"Oh, wow," he breathed as he took out a dark grey beanie with integrated headphones. "This is awesome! Thanks, sis. It's worth getting up for!" He ruffled Lauren's hair, and she felt her cheeks burn with pride.

There was one box left that was different from the empty, wrapped ones that Mum liked to keep under the tree, so it didn't look bare after all the gifts had gone. It was quite big, and Lauren was itching to know who it was for.

Mum reached towards it, a smile playing on her lips. "And now," she said, picking it up, "for your main present, Lauren."

"Me?" Lauren squealed, darting her a look of surprise. "But I've had loads. New leg warmers, books, that gorgeous lilac hoodie..."

"Well, this is a special present because Liam and I decided you need it." Mum handed over the box.

Lauren ripped off the wrapping to reveal a plain cardboard box that gave no hint of what was inside. With a grin, Liam handed her his penknife, and she sliced the Sellotape seals. Being very careful, she turned the box up and let the inner package slide out.

Then she gasped. "A laptop?" she whispered. "But... Mum, how can we afford that?" She tore at the box to get to the slimline computer inside and whistled in appreciation as she lifted it into the air and admired the sheen on the silver case.

"Nick chipped in," Mum admitted. "So, it's from him too."

Lauren continued admiring her new machine, saying nothing. Mum must be serious about Nick to let him be part of their Christmas. She'd even invited him to Christmas lunch and to spend the rest of the day with them.

"It's difficult to have a Saturday job when you're at boarding school," Liam broke into her thoughts. "So you could never save up for one on your own like I did."

Lauren darted him a grateful smile. "Yes, but Mum has to pay for all my uniform, and I seem to go through a lot of pointe shoes. I never expected... " Her voice faded away.

"Lauren, we're proud of you," Mum said, her voice breaking a little. "You're doing so well at Amberwood, and it's not as if I have to find the fees. You've kept your scholarship, and that's an enormous achievement. You deserve this."

Lauren uncoiled her legs and rose to her feet without using her hands. She put her arms round her mum's neck and hugged her tight. Tears were prickling her eyes, and she gave a gentle sniff. "Thank you," she whispered. "You know I'll look after it!"

Mum returned the hug. "Of course you will!" she said. "And I know you'll thank Nick properly too when he arrives. He promised he'd help you set it up."

But Lauren couldn't wait for that! She sat on the sofa with the instructions and plugged the laptop in to the nearest socket. She would make a start on her own.

The doorbell rang long before lunch and Nick arrived with even more parcels. Lauren looked up. She wasn't sure what Mum had meant when she'd said Lauren should thank Nick properly. Should she give him a kiss? Although she'd got to know him a bit better in the days leading up to Christmas, she wasn't sure if she was ready for that.

But she needn't have worried. Nick didn't seem to expect anything. He gave her a friendly grin and said, "I see you've got it going already?" and he sat beside her on the sofa to see how far she'd got.

Lauren turned the screen to face him. "I hope I've done it right," she said.

"Let's have a look," Nick replied and started clicking on keys that brought up all sorts of information that was gobbledegook to Lauren.

"Wow! You know what you're doing!" she laughed.

"Yeah, I've always been into IT," Nick replied, and he started explaining what he was doing. After a while, he said, "We can link this to the TV. Then, if you want to, you can download ballets or YouTube clips or whatever and watch them on a larger screen."

"That would be awesome," Lauren breathed. "Though even to watch them in my room, when everyone's watching something else on the TV, will be amazing."

For the next hour, Lauren and Nick worked on the laptop. Then Mum announced lunch was ready and the four of them sat round the festive table and laughed and joked their way through a scrumptious Christmas lunch. Lauren helped herself to seconds, and even thirds! It was so lovely to be able to eat heartily at home for the holidays. After all, it was Christmas! And she wasn't worried about gaining a bit of weight. She would soon burn it off once she got back to school and started training again.

In the end, she ate so much she felt she would burst. She would have to leave Christmas pudding till later.

Everyone mucked in with the clearing up and they spent the afternoon playing board games till Mum announced she was going to make a cup of tea. Nick followed her into the kitchen to help.

Lauren barely noticed them leaving. She was engrossed in the instructions for a new board game that Nick had brought with him. Each player was given a card with a category on it, such as flowers or types of job, and had to shout out as many associated words as possible in thirty seconds. This could be noisy, Lauren thought. She couldn't wait to play! Her and Liam against Mum and Nick. She began to lay out the board, then her tummy grumbled. Maybe she could fit that Christmas pudding in now.

Lauren stood up and went towards the kitchen.

"Have you asked them yet?" She heard Nick's voice, low and conspiratorial and she saw him standing near to the sink with Mum, his arms round her waist, staring into her flushed face. They sprang apart when they saw Lauren standing in the doorway.

"Asked who what?" Lauren said with a sinking feeling in her stomach.

"It's not what you think," Mum said quickly. Lauren frowned.

Nick held out his hand and took Mum's. Then he smiled at Lauren. "As Sam is too selfless to ask, I will," he said.

Lauren took half a step back. She wasn't sure she wanted to hear what Nick had to say. Was...was he going to ask her permission to *marry* Mum? She knew Mum had to make a new life, and it was great that she had company while Liam and Lauren were away at university and school, but it made Lauren feel lonely. She knew she should be happy for her mum, but she didn't want to share her yet.

"Lauren," Nick began, his voice sounding all formal and serious, "I'd really like to take your mum to a New Year's Eve ball at the officers' mess where my old squadron used to be. It's not far from here and they've invited loads of people I used to know. But your mum is reluctant to leave you alone. Would you mind terribly?"

Lauren wasn't sure whether she wanted to laugh or cry. Relief that this was nothing more serious than a night-out made her agree to Nick's request without a moment's thought.

"But I won't be alone, will I?" she said, looking at her mum. "Liam will be here. I'm sure we'll be fine. You should go, Mum."

Her mum beamed, and Lauren felt a tiny stab of guilt that Mum would even consider not going to a fancy party because of leaving her behind. She opened the fridge and took out the remains of the Christmas pudding and a tub of brandy butter. She put them on the counter and rummaged in the cupboard for a bowl. "I'll do your hair and make-up for the party if you like, Mum," she offered.

Her mum gave her a hug. "That would be amazing. But regular make-up, not stage paint, right?" she checked with a laugh.

Chapter Three

On New Year's Eve, Lauren picked up the TV remote and began to scroll through the channels, looking for something she and Liam could watch together. She had helped her mum with her hair and make-up and left her to get dressed.

"Well?" Mum's anxious voice sounded from the lounge doorway.

Lauren looked up. "Mum, you look stunning!"

Because Mum did. Lauren had swept her short, blonde hair to one side and sprinkled it with glitter. She'd given her a sweep of pale lilac eyeshadow and two coats of mascara, then coloured her cheeks with soft rose blush. Her mum's mauve evening dress hugged her slim figure and the pink and lilac rhinestone choker that formed the neck of the dress sparkled as much as the lights on the Christmas tree. Her face was radiant, and Lauren thought her own heart would burst with pride. She had the most beautiful mum in the world!

The doorbell rang and Mum opened it to let Nick in. Lauren was disappointed that he wasn't wearing RAF uniform.

"Well," Nick explained, "now that I'm retired, I'm no longer entitled to wear the uniform. It would be classed as 'impersonating an officer'. But we could have a fancy-dress dinner here at home one evening, if you like, and I'll put it on then."

"Cool!" said Lauren and high-fived him.

Five minutes later, Mum and Nick left in a flurry of instructions: "Be good. Don't open the door to strangers," at which Liam groaned, "Seriously?" and, "Go to bed at a reasonable time!"

Lauren breathed in a lungful of her mum's perfume that was lingering in the air after they'd gone and went back to scrolling through the TV channels.

"We could watch the latest Avengers movie," she suggested to Liam, who was pacing around the room. "Or how about a re-run of The Greatest Showman?" Her brother didn't answer. "Or we could search for something online?" Liam merely cracked his knuckles and gave a short, non-committal grunt.

"What's wrong?" Lauren asked, looking up at her brother. "You're very fidgety."

"I'm just fed up, that's all," Liam admitted. "It's all very well for them," he jerked his head towards the door through which Mum and Nick had just left, "but I wanted to go out too."

"Where did you want to go?" Lauren asked, intrigued. Liam hadn't mentioned this before.

Liam threw himself into an armchair. "All my mates from school are getting together at the High Voltage Club." He sighed. "It's the biggest reunion since we all went to uni. I hadn't got round to telling Mum that I wanted to go before she and Nick announced their plans. Then it felt mean to say anything." He stared moodily at the TV screen.

Lauren twirled the remote in her hands. "Well, you should go," she said.

"Don't be daft!" Liam tilted his head back and gazed at the ceiling. "I can't go out and leave you here all alone, can I?"

"Why not?"

Liam pressed his lips together and said nothing.

"Look," Lauren continued, "To be honest, there's nothing I'd love more than to watch Matthew Bourne's Swan Lake..."

"Is that the one where all the swans are men?" Liam interrupted.

"Yeah. But I know you wouldn't want to watch it. So, you'd be doing me a favour by going out. It would mean I could watch it on the TV, through my laptop, and really enjoy it."

"Well, you can do that anyway." Liam heaved himself to his feet. "I'll go upstairs and do some stuff on my own laptop."

"And where's the difference?" Lauren cried. "If you're hidden away upstairs, you might just as well be down the road at the club. What harm could I possibly come to, sitting here watching a ballet?"

Liam hesitated.

Lauren pressed her point. "I'll be perfectly happy, Liam. I'll lose myself so completely in the music and the dancing that you'll be back before I have time to miss you. Just get back before Mum does!" She tilted her head at her brother and made shooing motions with her hands.

Liam laughed. "Well, if you're absolutely sure..."

Lauren turned back to the TV. "Who is making that annoying noise in the background?" she asked the air.

Liam went to grab his coat off the rack in the hall, then came back to plonk a kiss on his sister's head. "You're ace, sis! I'll be back before Mum, don't worry. And don't open the door to anyone!"

Lauren stuck out her tongue and waved him away.

She smiled as the front door closed with a click. What bliss! She pulled a throw over her legs and snuggled into the cushions on the sofa while setting up the ballet to begin. Before she knew it, Tchaikovsky's famous music filled the room.

The ballet had just reached the first scene with the male swans when a sudden blast of cold air jolted Lauren out of her cocoon. She swivelled round to the sound of two voices yelling, "Surprise!"

And there, by the door, were the ghostly shapes of Grace and Rodney. Grace was beaming, and Rodney looked like he'd just pulled off the best trick in the world.

"Evenin', Miss Lauren!" he chortled, and he doffed his cap.

Lauren was so stunned, it took her a few seconds to speak. "What are you both doing here? How did you know I was on my own?"

"Well, we didn't. Not to start with," Grace admitted.

"Me an' 'er Grace was just going on a jaunt because we couldn't spend another minute in that 'spooky' old

Amberwood Hall." Rodney winked. "And we was bored with no students."

"We missed *you*!" Grace interrupted.

"We was only intending to spy on you a bit," Rodney continued, "but when we saw you was all alone, we decided to call in proper."

Lauren laughed. What a fabulous treat! She would have company after all, with two of her best friends in the world. "Ace!" she cried. "Let's have a party!" and she muted the TV with a quick flick of the remote.

"Whoa!" Rodney yelled. "How did you do that, Miss Lauren? Are you magic? Did you see that, Grace? She just made the telebox-thingy sound stop without touching it."

Grace rolled her eyes. "Seriously, Rodney? You've been a ghost for two hundred years. Don't tell me you've never seen a TV remote. What do you do with yourself when you're not at Amberwood?"

"'Orses don't have teleboxes in their stables, yer Grace," Rodney declared. "And that's where I spend all me time. So why should I know anything about it all? Go on, show me how it works, Miss Lauren."

Lauren showed Rodney the button that worked the volume. Then she left him practising pushing it without touching it, while she told Grace all about her Christmas presents. She had to keep raising and lowering her voice as the music blasted out or faded.

After a while, she and Grace stopped talking and turned to look at Rodney. He was glued to the TV screen, but he must have felt their gaze because he turned to face them. On the screen, Matthew Bourne’s all-male swans were bounding gracefully across the stage. Bare-chested with their legs covered in tights made of thick, white feathers, they looked powerful and menacing.

"How did I ever think ballet was just for girls or sissies?" he marvelled. "These chaps are amazing! They're so strong and... what's that modern word? Athletic!"

Lauren grinned. "Well, yes. Ballet is one of the most demanding physical disciplines. If you're so impressed, why don't we all sit down and watch it through?"

Rodney shook himself, like a dog shaking water off its coat. "Nah," he said, his admiration obviously exhausted. "Let's play a game!"

"Okay." Lauren looked at the pile of board games stacked in the corner of the room. The ghosts weren't going to be able to play any of those. Rodney could move things easily, but Grace struggled with small things. She could close doors and windows, or even swing the occasional latch, but shaking dice and moving tiny board game pieces would be difficult.

"How about Snapdragon?" Rodney suggested. "Didn't you used to play that in the parlour when you was a girl, Gracie?"

"What's Snapdragon?" asked Lauren, intrigued. She would love to learn a new game.

"You put raisins into a bowl of sherry, then light it," Grace said. "The idea is to pick the raisins out and eat them without getting burned!" Rodney folded his arms and nodded. "But I don't think that's a good idea, Rodney. The burning raisins will fall straight through us and singe the carpet. "

"No way!" Lauren exclaimed. "We're certainly not playing with fire. And anyway, I'm sure Mum used all the sherry in the trifle!"

"Well, what about Blind Man's Buff?" Rodney tried again. The girls shook their heads at him in despair.

"And how is Lauren supposed to feel for us?" Grace demanded. "Or how are we going to blindfold our eyes?"

"What about charades?" Lauren suggested. "Do you know that?"

Grace clapped her hands. "Oh, yes! We often used to play that when I was a girl." She looked at Rodney. "How many book titles do you know?"

The scruffy stable boy shrugged. "I knows the Bible."

Lauren instantly dismissed her ideas of TV programmes, films, or songs. This was going to be a different game of charades to the one she was used to. "Grace and I will take it in turns to give you a book title," she decided. "Then you'll have to act it to just one of us. Doesn't matter if you don't know the book. Just act out the words."

Rodney nodded, and Lauren explained how to play. "Hold up fingers to show how many words there are, and you can do this," she pulled her ear, "to say 'sounds like'. And this," she tapped three fingers on her arm, "shows which word you're describing, for instance, the third."

Rodney frowned. "Why would you act the third word first?" he questioned.

"Well, sometimes it helps people to guess," Lauren explained. "Shall I do the first one to show you?"

The ghosts nodded and Lauren racked her brains for a book that would have been around when Grace and Rodney were children. The oldest books she could think of were Alice in Wonderland and The Water Babies. But had they been written before 1820? She really didn't know. In the end she plumped for The Water Babies, then realised how incredibly difficult it was to act out those words.

"Rock-a-bye Baby!" Rodney yelled enthusiastically as Lauren mimed rocking a baby for the last word in the title. They all collapsed with laughter and Lauren told them the title, as they would never get it.

Rodney insisted on going next, and Grace whispered the title of a book into his ear. Within minutes, she and Lauren were laughing uncontrollably as Rodney pulled silly faces and tangled himself into knots that a contortionist would have envied.

Grace chose Dick Whittington and His Cat and made such a good job of it, Lauren could almost see the characters.

Then it was Lauren's turn again. She wondered if Jack and the Beanstalk had been a story in their time and thought she would go for it anyway. Rodney and Grace yelled out suggestions one after the other as Lauren tried to mime climbing a gigantic plant. She was so engrossed that she didn't notice they'd fallen quiet and Rodney was trying to send her a warning look, till she heard her mum's voice gasp, "What on earth are you doing?"

Lauren lowered her arms from above her head and put her foot back on the floor. The ghosts, with a sympathetic wave, vanished.

Lauren had to think quickly! Mum and Nick were standing in the doorway, staring at her as if she'd gone mad.

"I was practising something for drama class," she explained lamely. She threw covert glances around the room, disappointed that the ghosts had had to leave without saying goodbye!

Mum came further into the room and took off her coat. "Well, you did look comical," she said. "And I could hear you talking as we came through the door. I thought you were talking to Liam, but obviously not. Is he upstairs?" She went to the door and cocked her head towards the landing.

Lauren couldn't think what to say. She felt the colour drain from her face as her mum called out, "Liam?" before striding up the stairs. The bedroom door banged open, and Lauren winced. She glanced at Nick, and he lifted his shoulder in a half shrug.

Seconds later, Mum was back in the lounge, scarlet with anger.

"We came back early," she raged, "because I wanted to see the New Year in with my children. And thank goodness I did. If I'd known that Liam had gone out and left you all alone, I would have come back much sooner."

"But you didn't need to, Mum," Lauren protested. "I was fine, honestly. I was watching Swan Lake and then... then I decided to do some practice. I was happy. I didn't even notice Liam wasn't here."

"That's not the point," Mum snapped. "He betrayed my trust."

Nick took Mum's hand and gently turned her to face him. "I can understand you're angry, love," he said, "but no harm has been done, really. And I can remember what it was like to be nineteen and stuck at home when you want to be out with mates of your own age."

At that moment, they heard a key turning in the front door lock.

"Lauren!" Liam's voice called from the hall. "I'm back. I couldn't leave my little sis to bring the New Year in all alone, so I ca..." He appeared in the doorway and froze.

Mum was tapping her toe on the carpet and scowling at Liam. He grimaced and held out his hands in submission.

"I'm sorry, Mum," he mumbled. "I honestly haven't been gone long."

"And I made him go." Lauren stepped forward. "I could have phoned his mobile any time I wanted if I felt lonely, but I didn't. I'm absolutely old enough to spend an evening on my own. And if you want to know, I was enjoying it till you all appeared."

Mum looked from one to the other. The tenseness went out of her shoulders. "Oh my baby," she murmured, "you are growing up!" She pulled Liam and Lauren into a hug. "Just this once, I'll overlook it," she whispered into their ears. "But don't ever do it again!"

Liam grinned and squeezed them both. "I won't," he said.

"It's nearly midnight!" Nick announced. "Let's all join hands and sing Auld Lang Syne."

Lauren gave him her hand and took her mum's on the other side. She glanced furtively around the room. Were Grace and Rodney still here? Were they watching? She wished they could have joined in too.

As they sang the traditional song to greet the New Year, Lauren strained her ears. She thought she could just hear the ghosts singing in the distance.

Chapter Four

Katie was alone in the dorm, unpacking, when Lauren arrived back at school on the first day of term. They squealed and hugged before launching into accounts of the holidays, both speaking at once.

Every so often, Lauren glanced at Grace, who was hovering over the end of the bed, so she would feel included in the chat.

"I've no idea what she looks like," Lauren said in answer to Katie's question about Nyree. "I'm not even sure if it was her answering my emails. She sounded so grown-up. It was like I was getting emails from a senior." She continued shoving clothes into her drawers while she was talking. "Anyway, what about you and Ethan? Is he back? Have you seen him yet?"

Katie stopped unpacking and clutched a pile of leotards to her chest. "No, not yet. But he texted me almost every day. And he said he'd got me a present from New York. I can't wait to see him." Then she frowned and doubt clouded her face. "Actually, Laur, I'm a bit scared."

"What of?" Lauren stared at her friend in surprise.

"Well, I'm not sure my holiday news will be as interesting as his. How can a boring old Christmas in England match up to a glamourous two weeks in New York?"

"Oh, come on!" Lauren said. "What's that got to do with anything? You just said he texted you every day. I bet he's just as excited to see you. What does it matter if you haven't done anything extraordinary?"

At that moment, Allison clattered in, boasting to Emily about the expensive presents she'd got for Christmas. Three other girls were close behind and they all called out 'hi' as they heaved their cases onto their beds and started unpacking.

Lauren glanced at her watch and gasped. "Oh, no! I've got to go! Matron told me Nyree's taxi is due at five. I need to be in the entrance hall to meet her. I'm going to be late!" She hurriedly gathered the last few clothes that were strewn on her bed and threw them into a drawer. "You want to come with me?"

Katie gestured to the neatly folded clothes that were piled on her own bed. "I ought to finish this. You'll be bringing her up to the dorm anyway, won't you? Maybe it's better if I just wait here."

Lauren nodded. "Okay! See you soon." She glanced at Grace, who swooped up beside her.

"*Well, I'm certainly coming,*" Grace whispered, even though they both knew no one else could see or hear her.

Lauren pounded down the stairs and along the corridors while Grace floated effortlessly beside her. By the time they got to where they were going, Lauren was breathless. She skidded to a halt at the sight of Matron talking to tiniest girl Lauren had ever seen. She was smaller than the smallest Year Seven! Her head barely reached Matron's waist, and she was as delicate as a bird.

Grace remained in the shadows while Lauren crossed the open space of the entrance hall towards Matron and the girl. The pale grey and turquoise school uniform looked awesome against the girl's dark brown skin. Her hair was parted into individual squares like a chessboard across her head, each square containing a tiny knot of black hair tightly plaited.

"Sorry I'm a bit late, Matron," Lauren panted as she skirted around cases and stepped over bags to approach.

Matron turned with a smile. "Ah, here you are Lauren. This is Nyree!"

Nyree stared at Lauren with huge dark brown eyes that made Lauren feel like she was under a microscope.

"Show Nyree to the dormitory, Lauren. You can take some of her small bags. I'll get Mr Rowland to carry the big suitcases upstairs while we're at supper."

Lauren nodded and picked up a backpack and a holdall from the pile around Matron. "It's this way," she said, and she set off, back the way she'd just come. "How was the plane?"

"It was a Boeing 787-9 Dreamliner."

Lauren grinned. "No, I meant, how was your flight?"

"It was eleven hours and fifty-eight minutes," Nyree replied. "We cruised at 36,000 feet until sufficient fuel was burned for the plane to be light enough to rise to 40,000 feet where it flies more efficiently. We had two meals and five snacks."

Lauren stopped walking and her mouth fell open. This kid was clearly a brainiac! But she only questioned the one fact that had amazed her: "You were on the plane for twelve hours? Wow, you must have been dying to stretch your legs!"

"No," Nyree corrected, "eleven hours and fifty-eight minutes."

Lauren stared at her for a few seconds. "Okay," she drawled, darting a glance at Grace who was following at a discreet distance, then resumed her pace. She didn't know what to say. To cover her confusion, she started pointing out rooms to Nyree.

"This is the dining room. We'll come back here for supper as soon as we've dumped your bags. We all have supper together, but lunch is more casual and like a canteen. You can come and go according to your lessons or classes."

"They are synonyms," Nyree challenged.

"Sorry?"

"They mean the same thing," Nyree explained. "Lessons and classes."

"Oh, I see. Well, not in this case. Anything to do with performing we call classes, and ordinary schoolwork, lessons."

"So, 'lessons' for academia and 'classes' for artistry," Nyree stated, as though she were storing the information in a filing cabinet in her brain.

"Um, yeah, I guess!" Lauren agreed.

She steered Nyree up the stairs and along the landing to their dormitory. Katie and the others were still there, and they all looked round curiously when Lauren walked in. Grace drifted in and floated cross-legged two feet above Lauren's bed.

"Everyone, this is Nyree," Lauren announced. She swung Nyree's knapsack onto an empty bed. "This is your bed, Nyree. I'm right next to you, and Katie is on the other side of me."

Nyree had remained standing in the doorway. "I cannot sleep in a room with other people," she declared.

There was a ripple of laughter from the girls, but it was Katie who stepped in to help Lauren. "Hello, Nyree," she said kindly. "I'm Katie. We all sleep in dormitories. It really is good fun, you know."

"Yes, I'm afraid only prefects and seniors have their own rooms," Lauren chipped in.

Nyree folded her arms. "Then I shall be a prefect," she said.

Grace giggled. *"Get out of that one, Lauren,"* she called.

Nyree's eyes slid over the ghost and then immediately away. Grace's form froze, and Lauren held her breath, but Nyree didn't comment.

Lauren went back to the girl and tried to take her bag off her. "Nyree, please," she begged. "You can't be a prefect. You have to sleep in here with the rest of us. Please, just come in and unpack."

Nyree didn't move, and Lauren sighed. This mentoring business was proving a lot harder than she'd bargained for.

She wished Matron had chosen someone else to look after Nyree.

At that moment, Mrs Rowland, the deputy matron, walked up. "How's it going, girls? It's nearly suppertime. You should all be unpacked by now."

Lauren seized her opportunity and explained Nyree's argument.

Mrs Rowland looked down at the tiny girl and smiled. "Well, of course you can be a prefect, Nyree!" And she calmly relieved Nyree of her bag.

Lauren's eyebrows shot up to her hairline. She was about to protest when the deputy matron put the bag on the bed. "But first," she said, "you must complete Year Nine and Year Ten. And students in those years sleep in dormitories."

Nyree glared at her and seemed about to protest, but instead she gave a huge, shuddery sigh. "Very well," she said and, with dragging feet, approached the bed and undid the clasps on her bags.

Mrs Rowland headed for the door, a small smile playing about her lips.

Lauren stared after her, speechless.

Chapter Five

After supper, the Year Nines headed for the common room. Lauren desperately wanted to join in. She hadn't shown Katie her laptop yet, or caught up with all the boys' holiday news, but Nyree hadn't had time to unpack before supper and Matron insisted Lauren went back to the dormitory with her to help.

"You're as bad as Katie," Lauren grumbled as Nyree meticulously folded each garment. She refused to allow Lauren to throw everything into the drawers in her own haphazard way, or even help at all. So Lauren lay on her bed, texting her mum.

Eventually, Nyree finished and, each carrying their laptops, they went back downstairs to find the others.

Grace was drifting around the common room, listening in on people's conversations. She smiled and waved at Lauren, who gave a tiny nod back. Katie and Ethan were sitting on a sofa looking at photos on Ethan's phone. Mark and Jay were leaning over the back so that they could see too. Lauren headed straight for them and Katie looked up, her cheeks glowing. She pointed to her kit bag.

"Look what Ethan got me," she said. Clipped to the handle of her bag was a miniature pink satin pointe shoe charm.

"Wow," Lauren breathed. "It's gorgeous, Katie." She fingered the delicate satin of the shoe. It was a perfect miniature, right down to the pleats of satin under the pointe where it tucked under the leather back.

"And just look at this snow, Lauren," Katie prompted. "Show her Central Park, Ethan."

Ethan scrolled back and turned his phone to Lauren.

"It looks magical," she agreed. "What do you think, Nyree? I guess you don't see much snow in South Africa?"

"I've never seen snow in real life," Nyree admitted, staring at Ethan's photos. She reached out one brown finger, as if she might feel the crisp coldness of the snow on the screen.

"Well, you may yet! It's only January," Mark said, straightening his back. "Hey, cool laptop case!" He gestured to Nyree's bag, which had a striking geometrical pattern in browns, yellows, and oranges. "It looks like African art. I suppose you got it back home?"

Nyree withdrew her hand and looked down. "I did," she said, "but from an international online shop. It's not that special. I think you can get them anywhere."

A sudden burst of laughter came from the other side of the room where Allison and her friends were sitting. Alfie was sitting on the floor in the middle of the room, fiddling with some sort of gadget.

"Hey, Alfie," Allison called, "did you bring your ouija board back with you?"

Alfie looked up and grinned. "Better than that," he said, holding up the small black box. "Look what I got for Christmas!"

Allison leaned over to look. Intrigued, Lauren moved closer too.

"It looks like a TV remote," Allison remarked.

Alfie turned the gadget round to show it off. It was slim and black with a row of tiny coloured lights along the top, ranging from green, yellow, and amber to red.

"What is it?" Jay asked, abandoning his spot behind the sofa.

"It's an EMF detector," Alfie announced. "Electro Magnetic Force," he clarified at their blank looks.

"What does it do?" Nicola asked.

"It detects electric and magnetic resonances in the atmosphere," Nyree said before Alfie could speak.

"Well, of course!" Allison mocked. Nyree's gaze slid over Allison before settling back on Alfie.

"It detects ghosts!" Alfie crowed. "And I am going to use it to discover what kind of ghosts there are at Amberwood. Anyone who wants to join me can. We can start a ghost hunting society!"

At the mention of finding ghosts, Grace zapped over to float behind Lauren. *"I think Rodney needs to see this,"* she whispered in Lauren's ear and she vanished.

"Show us how it works then," Allison encouraged.

Alfie turned on the switch and the detector's lights all flashed up, then settled on green. "It's simple," he explained. "You just turn it on and scan around." He did a quick sweep of the common room. The lights remained green. "Looks like there's nothing in here."

Lauren swallowed her unease. The detector was correct, there weren't any ghosts in here at the moment, but what if it worked when Grace and Rodney were around? As far as Lauren knew, they had managed to stay hidden for 200 years! Was Alfie about to ruin it all for them?

"You should try the clock tower in the stable block, mate," Jay suggested. "Don't you remember last term? Ethan thought he saw a ghost there?"

Ethan and Katie looked up from their spot on the sofa. Lauren held her breath, but Ethan shrugged. "I think we were just super hyped up," he said. He and Katie came over to the group.

"Anyway," Mark added, "the clock tower has been boarded up after your adventures last term." And he gave Ethan a friendly punch on the arm.

Lauren breathed a sigh of relief. Then Allison ruined it.

"Lauren, didn't we see a ghost at the end of last summer's term? In the old attic studio?" She half closed her eyes as if trying to visualise the event. "Wasn't she called Grace?"

The blood drained out of Lauren's face, and she thought quickly. She didn't want to tell a lie, but she had to put Allison off the scent. At the time, Grace had assured her that Allison wouldn't remember anything, but obviously she did.

Pretending to rub an itch on her back, Lauren crossed her fingers. Then she pursed her lips and inclined her head, like she was trying to remember the incident.

"Um, I don't remember seeing any ghost," she said. "All I remember is guiding you back from the attic studio when you were sleep-walking."

Allison frowned. "It's very hazy," she murmured, "but I remember something. Maybe it was a dream!"

Alfie grabbed her arm in excitement. "Don't you see?" he enthused. "That's one of the ways ghosts lure you: through dreams! We should check out this old studio first."

"You can't," Lauren declared. "The only way to get to it is off the landing from the girls' dormitories, and you're not allowed upstairs in the main house." She raised her voice slightly so everyone could hear. "Look guys, this is silly. There aren't any ghosts at Amberwood. Who has ever felt spooked?"

Nyree shot Alfie a curious glance. "What are you going to do if you find any?" she asked. "Invite it to tea?"

Everyone chuckled. Alfie grinned. "No, but if it's an evil spirit, there are ways to get rid of it. I've been researching stuff all over the Christmas holidays. I'll help it leave."

"And what if it's a friendly spirit?" Nyree argued.

Alfie brushed his blonde hair off his forehead and sighed. "Let's just find one first, shall we? I'm going to spend some time in the library researching sudden deaths at Amberwood through the years. Spirits always linger where they died," he finished importantly.

Jay let out a loud laugh. "You? You're going to open a book and study?" he teased.

Alfie shrugged. "No, there's an old dinosaur of a computer in there that no one ever bothers with. As I don't have my own laptop, like some..." He stared pointedly at

Nyree and Lauren, "and the ones in the computer room are always busy, I'll use that."

Lauren guessed he was waiting for her to say he could borrow her laptop, but she kept quiet. To her relief, so did Nyree.

Mrs Rowland came in. "How about we get to bed early tonight, folks?" she suggested. "Some of us have had long journeys," she glanced at Nyree, "and tomorrow will be a very full day."

People drifted away, picking up their belongings and heading out. The boys pulled on jackets and hoodies for their walk across the grounds to their dormitories in the stable block.

Lauren watched Alfie as he strolled away, chatting to anyone who would listen about the methods he had found for discovering ghosts. Her stomach felt like lead. Did these things really work? Would Alfie find Grace and Rodney and make trouble for them? The leaden feeling grew as she followed Katie, Nyree, and the other girls up the stairs to their dormitory.

Chapter Six

All eyes were on Nyree in the first ballet class of term. Everyone was curious to see what sort of dancer she would be. And Grace was the most curious. She perched in her usual place on the corner of the piano and watched the students file in, leave their pointe shoes and water bottles by the resin box, and hang their towels over the barre supports.

It must be quite daunting, Grace thought as she watched Nyree position herself between Lauren and Katie, to be new in the middle of the year. She must know that everyone would try to watch her. But the little girl didn't seem bothered. She settled precisely into first position, sideways to the barre, with one arm forming a semi-circular frame against her body in *bras bas* and the other placed on the bar. While everyone else was chatting and warming up prior to Mr Holt's arrival, Nyree stood perfectly still, waiting.

Even when Mr Holt rushed in and took the register, Nyree didn't break her stance. Her face was solemn and serene, as though she was concentrating intently on what she was about to do. As the first bars of music filled the studio, Grace winked at Lauren who, in contrast to Nyree's serious expression, was glowing with the sheer pleasure of doing what she loved best.

Grace couldn't fault Nyree's technique. Every movement was accurate, her feet never missed a position. She wasn't overly supple, but her balance was uncanny. She stood on *demi-pointe* on one foot at the end of an *adage* exercise, and there wasn't even the tiniest ripple in the muscles of her ankle and feet to show that they were adjusting to hold her there. She was like a rock! She even took off her crossover cardigan while maintaining the central point of balance which others were struggling to find at all.

But why doesn’t she smile? Grace wondered. Any other student would be delighted by such a display of control. Nyree’s face didn’t change. She didn’t look sad, but neither did she look as though she was enjoying herself. Others grimaced in pain because they were stiff after the holidays, or tried unsuccessfully to hide smiles of satisfaction when praised by Mr Holt, but Nyree’s face remained expressionless.

Maybe she's homesick, Grace mused. That would explain a lot. And would be totally understandable for such a young girl. How overwhelming it must be, travelling so far, all alone, and joining a school where everyone else already knew each other. Grace decided she would hold her judgment until Nyree had settled in a bit.

Nyree was just as controlled when they came into the centre of the studio. Mr Holt put her in the front row and she picked up the new exercises that he set for them really quickly. Her pirouettes were perfect, and she finished each one without a single wobble.

In allegro though, fast exercises with a lot of jumps, she wasn't so agile. Despite being so tiny, she didn't get very far off the floor when she jumped.

All too soon, the class ended, and Mr Holt held up his hand for attention before everyone left.

"Don't forget we've got the House Choreographic Competition this term," he announced. "The House captains will hold auditions for parts at the weekend, and you're all expected to try out."

A buzz of excitement filled the room.

"Not everyone will be taking part." Mr Holt raised his voice above the chatter, which stopped instantly. He turned to Jay. "Sorry Jay, but you mustn't do any dancing unless supervised by a dance teacher. We don't want you ruining all the healing you've done for your leg by one false movement."

Jay's shoulders sagged, but he gave a wry smile and nodded. Mr Holt had only allowed him to do the first few barre exercises, then made him sit down and watch the rest of the class.

"What did you say last term, about me dancing in the next show?" he whispered to Lauren as they all filed out. She squeezed his arm in sympathy.

"It sucks," she agreed, "but it's better than doing damage and missing out on something more important. After all, this is only in-house. Not even parents will be coming to watch, from what I heard. It's not such a big deal!"

"And there's no guarantee we'll all get parts anyway," Katie added, coming up behind them with Ethan. "It'll depend on what each House does. I heard a rumour that

Hazel Woodley was considering choreographing a *pas de deux* for Sylphides House."

"She can't do that!" Alfie, who was ahead, turned round, his face aghast. "I'm the only Year Nine boy in Sylphides and I was banking on a part!"

"We're all the only Year Nine boys in our houses," Mark pointed out. "There are only four of us and four Houses!"

"Oh yeah, you're right," Alfie conceded.

Katie shrugged. "It was only a rumour, anyway."

"Shall we go to the canteen for morning break?" Lauren suggested, directing her question at Katie, Ethan and Jay as Mark and Alfie bounded away up the stairs.

Katie shook her head. "Sorry. I've got a meeting with the school magazine committee. I'll have to catch you later."

"I'll walk you," Ethan offered, and they arranged to meet outside the stable block in ten minutes, after they'd got changed.

Lauren turned to Jay.

"I can't either," he said. "I've got an appointment to see the physio." He waved as he followed the other boys upstairs to the dormitory.

Lauren eyes widened and she looked at Grace, who grinned at her.

"You've still got Nyree," she pointed out, though she could see the disappointment in Lauren's eyes. Lauren was so used to doing everything with Katie. It must be hard for her to see her friend preoccupied with someone else.

Nyree moved closer to the older girl and stared up at her. "Do they have orange juice in the canteen?" she asked.

"What? Oh, er, yes, of course." Lauren straightened her shoulders. "Come on. We'll get changed and I'll show you the way."

"I remember the way," Nyree declared. "Yesterday you told me it's in the dining room where we had supper last night and breakfast this morning."

Lauren sighed. "Yeah. I did."

"But I would still like us to go together," Nyree continued. "Matron said I should stick with you."

"I don't think she meant constantly," Lauren pointed out, her voice betraying her growing impatience.

But Nyree just gazed at Lauren with her piercing eyes.

Chapter Seven

The two girls headed for the main house with Grace floating slightly behind them. As they passed the common room door, Lauren heard a lot of giggling and shushing. Then a different sort of cackle that made Grace cry out in alarm.

"Rodney! I'd better see what's going on." And she melted through the wall.

Lauren turned to Nyree. "Sounds like there's some fun going on in there. Shall we go and see?" she suggested.

"Of course," Nyree agreed.

Lauren pushed open the door. Grace was already inside and floating towards a group of Year Eight and Nine girls who had gathered round Alfie. Rodney, a huge grin plastered over his face, was hovering in mid-air behind the boy, peering over his shoulder. Lauren and Nyree went closer to listen.

"If there's a ghost present," Alfie was explaining, "the red light will flash and the detector will make a high-pitched whine." He turned the dial on the detector and pointed it to the far corner.

Rodney screwed up his face and pushed his fingers into the bulbs, jamming them all before there was any chance they might work. Only the green one remained lit. *"It doesn't appear to be working, mate!"* he chortled.

Lauren hid a grin, and Grace tutted at the stable boy. Alfie continued to sweep the room, oblivious to the fact that he was swinging a ghost along with him. Rodney splayed his legs and spare arm as though parachuting.

"Wheeeee!" he shouted as he flew.

"So," Alfie continued, "as you can see, there's nothing here. But I can give you the detector and you can go upstairs and try it in the attic studio."

He turned the device off and handed it to Allison. The rest of the girls clamoured round, claiming they could go before the bell went for lessons.

Rodney was rubbing his hands in glee, and Grace swooped over to him, grabbed his ear, and pulled him away behind Nyree. *"Leave it be!"* she admonished.

Lauren glanced at the two ghosts. Then, hoping everyone would think she was talking to Nyree, she spoke to the air above the girl's head.

"It might be better if you don't come," she said.

Nyree glanced at the wall behind her, then looked back at Lauren, her expression unreadable.

"Getting tired of mentoring already, Lauren?" said Allison, her mouth curving into a mocking smile. "Though I don't blame you."

Nyree's eyes widened, and her jaw tightened.

Lauren snapped to her defence. "There's no need to be mean, Allison!"

"Well, it was your call first!" Allison retorted and swept towards the door with the device and the other girls.

"I could go and do some homework, or ballet practice, if you want?" Nyree murmured.

Lauren sighed. "No, I'm sorry. I didn't mean it. Let's not give Allison the satisfaction. Come on. I want to see what happens." She glared at Rodney, who was arguing with Grace on the other side of the room.

Lauren and Nyree caught up with the other girls at the top of the main stairs. They clattered along the corridor, all talking at once, but slowed when they got to the narrow, dark staircase that led to the attic studio.

"I've never been up here before," whispered a Year Eight girl, hanging back.

Allison was still leading the way. She pushed open the door and it creaked louder than Lauren remembered. Had Rodney got away from Grace? Lauren had no idea whether Alfie's device would work or not, but if Rodney was in the studio, it would be better if she got it off Allison, just in case.

Another Year Eight, further up the line, squealed and pushed past everyone to get back down the stairs. "I'm not going," she shuddered. "It's too spooky!"

Allison peered round the half open door, hesitating. Taking her opportunity, Lauren ran up the stairs and pulled the detector out of Allison's hand.

"Here," she said firmly, "let me go first."

She pushed the door fully open. It was just as she remembered. The framed mirrors on the walls had mottled rusty marks all over them. And the old barres sagged in the middle. Dust rose in a swirl and glistened in the sunlight coming through the only window, high in the rafters. Everyone craned their necks to look in.

Nicola screamed, "A ghost!" and half the girls turned tail and clattered back down the stairs to escape.

The remaining ones piled into the room behind Lauren. In the middle of the swirling dust, she could see the faint outline of Rodney doing a silly sort of mad caper. Despite being cross with him for disobeying her and Grace, Lauren had to bite the inside of her cheek to stop herself from laughing. She kept the 'on' switch of the device firmly held to 'off'.

Rodney grinned at her, and she rolled her eyes at him.

"See, there's no ghost," she said aloud, as she waved the detector round the room. She coughed pointedly. "Just an awful lot of dust that we've disturbed. It's so musty in here. I think we should get out."

There were murmurs of agreement. Some sounded disappointed, though most were clearly relieved. They turned and trooped back to the common room.

Ethan, Jay, and Katie looked up expectantly as the girls piled into the room.

"Well?" Alfie prompted, holding his hand out for his detector.

Grace, who had been swishing up and down in agitation, aimed a questioning glance at Lauren.

"Nothing," Allison reported, as though she had been the one doing the detecting.

Alfie blew out his cheeks. "Well, I'm sort of glad," he said. "It would have been a real bummer if there had been a ghost somewhere I can't go!" He took the detector from Lauren and shoved it into his bag, which he hitched onto his shoulder. "I'm going to the library to see what I can find. If I can discover the exact location where someone died, we could target better."

"I don't think you've got time," Lauren warned. "The bell will go soon." She flashed Grace a half smile of comfort and the ghost drifted away, murmuring soft threats against Rodney.

Lauren turned to Katie. "How did the committee meeting go?"

Katie's face was glowing, and she looked like she'd just won the star part in a show. "Brilliant! This morning, in class," she said excitedly, "I had a brainwave. I didn't want to tell you till I'd passed it by the committee, but they're all for it!"

"Well, come on! Spill!" Lauren urged.

Katie looked round them all, savouring the moment. "I came up with this idea of starting a Gossip Wall on the magazine's online pages. I know there's already pages to upload dance diaries, competition results and show reviews etc, but this would be totally informal. Just chit chat about what's going on. Or it could be a good place to ask if someone's lost something..."

"Or wants to give something away," Ethan suggested.

Katie beamed at him. "Exactly! Anything really. People could say more about what they like. In the canteen, for instance!"

"More chocolate cake!" Jay cried.

Everyone laughed.

"Anyway, the editors loved the idea. I just need to work out how to set it up."

"I could help," Mark offered. He was hovering on the fringe of their group, looking like he wanted to join in. "It's not that difficult."

Katie smiled at him. "That would be awesome! If you really don't mind. Because I actually don't know where to start."

"It'd be easier to do it on a PC. Shall we grab one in the computer room after supper?" Mark suggested.

Katie nodded. "As long as I get all my homework done first," she sighed. "Maths! Who in their right mind invented maths!"

"The ancient Sumarians in Mesopotamia, 3000 BC," stated Nyree.

Everyone stared at her.

Nyree stared back and lifted her chin. "It's my favourite subject," she declared.

Just then, the bell rang, shattering the moment.

"Double history," Lauren groaned, and she yawned and stretched. Out of habit, she looked towards Katie so they could walk together. But Katie was already heading for the door with Ethan.

Lauren swallowed. Then she felt Nyree's eyes on her and she straightened her shoulders. "Maybe we can get Mrs Rowe to tell us something about the history of Amberwood Hall," she rallied. "That'll keep Alfie happy!"

Chapter Eight

On Saturday afternoon, everyone gathered at the stable block studios for the House Cup auditions. Each House had taken one of the four studios and the captains were busy inside making their preparations. The rest of the students were filling every other corner of the building trying to warm up. Girls ran their legs up walls in splits, instruments were moved in the music rooms to make floor space for stretching, and the corridors were heaving with students contorting their bodies or merely lounging against the walls. Everyone was chatting and speculating and calling out encouragement or teasing one another. The noise was deafening.

"PIPE DOWN!" came a thunderous roar from the door of Studio Two. Julian Morgan, Head Boy and Spartacus Captain, glared round the assembled students. Gradually, the noise quietened, and he waved a hand. "Go to your allotted studios. Your captains will explain how it's all going to work." And he retreated into the room.

Lauren and Nyree filed into the studio behind him, along with Susie Lo Hin and Claire Carter from their year. Lauren crossed her fingers, hoping whatever theme Julian had chosen would need a lot of dancers. She glanced up at Grace, who was floating beside her, keeping her promise to Lauren to come and cheer her along. Jay had come too, though only to watch.

As they spread out into the studio, everyone stared at signs that were sellotaped to the walls at three metre intervals: TEDDIES, JACK-IN-A-BOX, TOY CATS, CLOWN PUPPET, TOY SOLDIERS, FAIRY DOLL.

Intrigued, they all sat on the floor against the full-length mirrors and waited impatiently for Julian to tell them what he had in store.

The Head Boy stood in the middle of the studio with Helena Markova, also in Year Eleven, and rustled a sheaf of papers. "So," he started after he'd cleared his throat. "We've decided to do a ballet about a toy shop where all the toys come to life."

"A well-trodden path for ballets," Grace whispered into Lauren's ear.

"Hardly original!" Lauren muttered back, then pulled a face when Nyree turned questioning eyes to her. Lauren shrugged. She shouldn't judge too quickly. Maybe Julian had an out-of-the-box slant on the popular theme.

But as he outlined the parts available, the piece sounded more and more like a cross between Copélia and The Nutcracker. Lauren's excitement dwindled.

She whispered behind her hand to Jay. "I'm not sure I want to try out for anything. After all, who wants to be a teddy bear, a toy cat, a jack-in-a-box or a clown puppet? It looks like Julian and Helena have already claimed the only decent parts, the toy shop owner and his daughter."

"There's always the fairy doll," Jay whispered back. "That might be quite classical." He didn't sound convinced though.

"Everyone," Julian called, "stand under the sign showing whatever you want to audition for, and we'll do one group at a time. We'll start with teddy bears."

Everyone stood up and rearranged themselves underneath the appropriate signage. The boys claimed the jack-in-a-box spot, but nearly all the girls headed for Fairy Doll. Nobody chose toy cats, clown puppet, soldiers or teddy bears.

Julian frowned. "This is no good," he muttered. He and Helena retreated to a corner and had a whispered conversation. Then Julian came back, running his hand through his hair. "Right," he said, "we'll do it differently. You'll all audition for everything, and *we'll* choose who dances what part."

"Stand behind me, everyone," Helena called. She outlined the steps, and the audition got under way.

After a gruelling hour and a half of dancing various combinations, Julian and Helena told everyone to rest while they made their decisions.

In the end, Nyree got the part of the fairy doll.

"You're just so amazing at standing still!" Julian complimented her. "And we're going to have to carry you around a lot, so it helps that you're so small."

Lauren thought Nyree was actually going to smile. The corners of her mouth lifted slightly and her eyes brightened. But in the end, she just nodded solemnly. Lauren was pleased for her, but also disappointed: it seemed to be the only part that was going to be danced *en pointe*.

"Lauren Mason," Lauren held her breath. "We've chosen you for the clown puppet."

Julian continued down the list. Lauren sighed. Well, at least she had got a solo. Apart from the fairy doll and the jack-in-a-box, the other parts were groups. She would just have to be the best clown puppet ever!

Julian ended by giving the chosen ones the rehearsal schedule and then dismissed them.

"Sorry we couldn't use everybody," he called as they grabbed their towels and water bottles and headed for the changing rooms.

Back in the common room, the noise was almost as deafening as it had been in the stable block. Lauren scanned the room. All around, people were comparing notes, discussing what parts they had landed or, in the case of some, bemoaning the fact that they hadn't got a part at all. Though it was easy to pick out the people who had, from their happy expressions and slight air of superiority. Allison was holding court on the other side of the room, and clearly gloating to have been the only Year Nine chosen for her House, Bayadere.

Lauren, shadowed by Nyree, made a bee-line for Katie and Ethan, who were talking to Mark, Jay, and Alfie.

Lauren nodded at Ethan. "If you smile any wider, your face will crack. You obviously got a part."

For an answer, Ethan did a complicated series of movements with his hands that flowed into his arms through his torso and ended in a crouched spin.

Katie rolled her eyes. "He didn't just land a part," she said, clearly pleased. "The whole thing is based round him and his unique style of acro-dance. He IS the choreography!"

"Wow!" Lauren breathed. "That's something. I wish I was in Carmen."

Katie snorted. "Well, I wish I wasn't! My modern dance isn't strong enough. I didn't get a part at all."

"Neither did I," said Mark, though he didn't seem too bothered. "You and I can hang out, Katie, while everyone else is rehearsing!"

"Oh, I'll be very busy monitoring the new Gossip Wall," Katie declared. "I'm going to throw myself into my role at the *En Pointe* magazine. But thanks for helping me create the page," she added hurriedly.

"Speaking of point," Lauren grumbled. "I'm not even getting to dance *en pointe*. I'm a clown!" She told Katie about Julian's plans for the piece.

Katie winced. "Hm, it sounds..."

"Old fashioned," Lauren interrupted. "Unless he's got some very unique ideas tucked up his sleeve."

"I wonder if he'd be open to suggestions?" Jay offered, perched on the arm of the sofa. "At least you and Ethan have got parts, Lauren." He grimaced a little as he eased his injured leg. "I've got to do special training sessions with Mr Holt while you're all enjoying yourselves."

"How about you, Alfie?" Lauren tilted her head at Alfie. "Is Hazel doing a pas de deux for Sylphides House?"

Alfie nodded. "She is. There is a corps too, but they chose Year Ten and up. I'm not dancing!" He stood up. "You can sit here if you want, Jay. I'm going to the library." And he strolled away.

Ethan gave Lauren a mock punch in the arm. "Looks like it's just you and me dancing in the House Cup then!"

Katie darted him a quick look of surprise just as Nyree piped up, "And me!"

Chapter Nine

The next Sunday afternoon, Lauren sat in the library, pretending to do some homework. In reality, she was monitoring Alfie. Grace had come to her in quite a flurry, saying she was afraid he might find out too much. So Lauren had agreed to keep watch, along with the ghosts.

Nyree, Lauren's constant companion, was sitting opposite her and Rodney was flitting around the room, making her feel dizzy. Grace hovered by the window, twisting the lace on her petticoats.

"You don't have to worrit, Yer Grace, Miss Lauren," Rodney called. *"Every time 'e finds summat,"* Rodney cocked a thumb towards Alfie, *"I freeze 'is computer."* And to prove his point, he swooped through the monitor and out the other side.

Alfie groaned and said a bad word under his breath. Then he looked round guiltily in case a prefect or member of staff had heard him. But there was no one else in the library apart from Nyree and Lauren. His eyes locked with Nyree's.

"Would you like to borrow my laptop?" she offered, and she picked the multi-coloured bag up off the floor.

"Nice case!" Alfie commented.

Nyree blew out her cheeks. "I already told Mark, it's nothing special. There are plenty more online if you want one."

At that moment, the door flew open and Katie, flushed and panting, rushed in, holding her own laptop open. She pushed onto the seat next to Lauren and pointed to the screen.

"Just look at this," she cried, totally ignoring the "Be Silent" signs on the walls. "I found it on the Gossip Wall."

Lauren looked where Katie was pointing and read out the post:

"*It's all right for some... Just because Ethan Tern got private lessons during the holidays in NEW YORK, he's getting an entire choreography built round him. Let's hope the stage is big enough for his head.*"

"That's monstrous!" Lauren gasped. "And there's no name. Just a row of numbers and symbols."

"And that avatar of a detective," Katie pointed out. "But you're right. There's nothing to show who sent it. It's anonymous."

"Who would say such a nasty thing?" Lauren continued. "And why shouldn't Ethan want to improve his dancing? Isn't that what we're all here to do?"

Katie nodded glumly.

"You're the administrator." Nyree put down her pen and looked directly at Katie. "That means you have the power to delete it."

"You can't do that!" Alfie peered round from behind his screen. "Freedom of speech!"

Katie pressed her lips together. "What do you think, Lauren?"

Lauren frowned. "I think it's a one-off nasty comment from someone who's just jealous. You should ignore it. Look, there's loads of really interesting posts to take attention off it. What about this one from Alyssa Shears, Year Eight?"

She positioned the computer screen at an angle and read: "*I heard strange noises coming from the cellar yesterday evening as I was passing the entrance*".

"Ha! That was me!" crowed Rodney, doing a fly past above their heads. Lauren ignored him.

"Or this one," she continued. "*Has anyone noticed how the Choreographics Cup, locked in a cupboard, keeps moving*? That's from Caleb Clark, Year Ten."

"Me again!" Rodney cackled.

Alfie came over to look at the screen. "That's brilliant!" he breathed. "People are sitting up and taking notice of paranormal activity."

The door flew open once more, and this time Jay and Ethan came striding in. Katie closed her laptop quickly and smiled at Ethan.

"So this is where you're all hiding," he said.

"Jay! Just the man!" Alfie cried, thumping Jay on the back. "Remember how you picked the lock to the tower last term?"

Jay hesitated. "Yeah, but it's boarded up this term. I can't do it again."

"Don't want you to, mate." Alfie grinned. "I want you to pick the lock on the House Cup cupboard. We've just read a rumour on the Gossip Wall that the cup is moving, INSIDE THE LOCKED CUPBOARD!"

"Now look what you've done," Grace scolded Rodney, who did a somersault in mid-air and chortled happily.

Oblivious, Alfie continued. "I want to draw a chalk line around the base of the cup. Then we'll be able to see if it really is moving."

"Okay," Jay agreed. "Sounds like a challenge. I am a bit bored!" He gestured to the computer where Alfie had been sitting. "Have you got anything yet?"

Alfie scooted back to his place and scrolled a bit. "There's some interesting stuff," he said. "Apparently, in the 1800s, two children died within a week of each other. Surely their ghosts will be around somewhere?"

Grace's hand flew to her mouth and she gave a faint groan. Lauren leaped up and went over to the computer.

"Let's see that," she said, a bit too forcibly. Her eyes scanned the page. "It says they both died in the grounds," she declared. "So, even if there were any ghosts, they're not likely to be in the house, are they? Certainly nowhere near the cellar. And if you really want to spend hours outside in this weather, you're on your own!"

"It's worth a quick scan with the detector," Alfie argued.

Grace groaned again. *"Do something, Lauren!"* she cried, flying round and round the room at speed.

"I really think you should stop digging," Lauren tried, her voice verging on desperation.

"Why?" Alfie's eyes narrowed. "Are you scared?"

Rodney burst out laughing at that, and Grace rounded on him. *"This is all your fault,"* she seethed. *"If you had left well alone, and not gone around stoking the rumours, he'd have forgotten all about searching for us."*

The corners of Rodney's mouth turned down for a moment. Then they turned up again just as quickly, and he waggled his eyebrows. *"I think it's a great lark!"* he chortled.

"You won't think that if they find us and then bring in professionals to get rid of us," Grace fumed. Her entire form

was sparking like two electric cables accidentally touching each other.

"Don't take on so, yer Grace," Rodney comforted. *"We can always skedaddle for a few days if they do that. No one will find us!"*

Ethan shivered. "Is it me, or has it gone cold in here?" he asked.

Lauren darted him a look. Ethan had been sensitive to the ghosts' presence last term. And Rodney had made things worse then. She had to stop the ghosts arguing. She tried to catch Grace's eye, but Grace was still glaring at Rodney and didn't look her way.

"C'mon, Katie," Ethan said, to Lauren's relief. "I can think of nicer places to spend a Sunday afternoon than this spooky old library and all this talk of ghosts. Let's go for a walk." He put his hand on Katie's shoulder and she stood up, ready to leave.

Lauren wondered if she should suggest they all go, or would that cramp Katie's style? She was about to speak when her mobile pinged. She fished it out of her pocket and read the message.

"Hey, wait," she called to Ethan and Katie, who had reached the door. "It's a text from Lizzie, from the local school. Remember, we did that choreography for the YouTube competition with her last term?"

"What does she say?" Katie asked.

Lauren looked back at her phone. "Their school is putting on a Valentine's Day party and she's asking if our Years Nine and Ten would be allowed to go."

Immediately, the atmosphere in the room lightened as the static that Grace was creating subsided. She floated nearer to Lauren to get a look at the text.

Ethan let go of the door and he and Katie stepped back inside.

"That would be awesome," Jay said. "Do you think Mrs Herriott will let us?"

"I think she might if Katie asks," Ethan said with a proud smile in Katie's direction.

"Katie gets my vote," Jay declared, and Alfie and Nyree nodded their agreement.

"No time like the present." Katie grinned. "But I vote we all go together. I'll be spokesperson."

Everyone gathered up their belongings and joined Katie and Ethan at the door.

Lauren looked back at Grace, whose face was glowing. She was floating by the window, her hands clasped to her chest and her eyes all dreamy.

"Ah, romance!" She sighed. *"I never got a Valentine's card!"* She smiled at Lauren. *"Perhaps thoughts of love might take their minds off ghost-hunting."*

Rodney tutted his disgust. *"Just when we was having fun."*

Chapter Ten

The following Saturday, after the first rehearsal for the choreographics competition, Lauren went to the common room in search of Katie. She found her friend sitting cross-legged on a sofa, tapping away at her laptop. A few other people were dotted around the room, but on the whole it was quiet. Those who didn't have to attend rehearsals had gone into town or were catching up on homework.

With a huge sigh, Lauren threw herself down next to Katie. Nyree perched on the arm of the sofa and Katie looked from one to the other.

"Have you seen Ethan?" she asked. "He said he'd be finished at rehearsal by now."

Lauren shrugged. "No. He didn't walk up with us," she said, looking round the common room. "I don't know where he went. The canteen, maybe?"

Katie nodded. "How did your rehearsal go?" she asked.

"Quite boring, really!" Lauren complained.

Katie grinned. "How could it be boring? There’s nothing you love more than dancing, Lauren. Surely any type of dancing is better than none?"

"Well, it would be if we did anything," Lauren argued. She picked up a cushion and started pulling at the fringing around the edge. "I didn't even break a sweat! You know how, with Mr Holt, he has all the routines worked out in advance?"

Katie nodded.

"Well, Julian doesn't seem to have a clue what he wants to do," Lauren continued. "He's working it out as he goes along, and we spent most of the time standing around doing nothing."

"Why does waiting make you cross?" Nyree ventured. "It's a good time to think. And aren't you pleased Julian has changed some toys since Jay suggested it? Robots and aliens are much more contemporary than toy soldiers and teddy bears."

"Yes, but I'm still a clown," Lauren grumbled.

Suddenly Katie gasped. She went bright pink and when Lauren looked at her enquiringly, she pointed to her screen. "There's another post from the anonymous detective," she whispered.

Lauren leaned over and read out loud.

"Isn't Ethan Tern supposed to be Katie Dansfield's boyfriend? He seems to spend a lot of time with Lauren Mason..."

Lauren slammed the lid of the laptop down. "What sort of rubbish is that?" she cried. "Of course we walked over to the stable block together. Why wouldn't we? After that, we were in separate studios."

Katie bit her lip. "I know. It's stupid. Just malicious gossip."

"Anyway," Lauren continued to fume, "Nyree was with us too. When isn't she?" she finished sourly.

Nyree flinched as though she'd been stung and Lauren flushed. She hadn't meant to hurt the girl's feelings.

"You're forgetting the afternoon break when Ethan was teaching you some of his moves," Nyree commented. "Maybe the 'Secret Detective' saw you then."

Lauren glanced at her uneasily.

"Or what about last Wednesday?" Nyree continued, "when you, rather than Katie, were helping him with his English essay? After all, English is Katie's special subject."

Katie's eyes flicked between them and Lauren felt the blood rush into her face. Was Nyree deliberately trying to make Lauren look bad? "Don't be silly," she said. "And it wasn't an essay, it was a summary. I'm good at those!"

Nyree shrugged. "You did have your heads quite close together."

"We can still be friends, can't we?" Lauren cried. She sent Katie a pleading look. "There was nothing else to it. Instead of arguing, we should find out who's spreading these horrible rumours."

Katie nodded. "I agree," she said, and she opened the laptop again to study the offending post. "It was posted at 2 a.m." She rubbed her temples. "Who on earth is around at that time of night? We're not allowed our phones after lights-out. So it had to be done on a laptop."

Lauren made a mental note to get Grace and Rodney to patrol the school at night. Maybe they could catch this miserable specimen and give him or her the fright of their lives.

Nyree chipped in. "Messages can be scheduled to be sent at a later time," she suggested. "And from any computer, really."

People drifted in and the room slowly filled. Nyree gestured around. "Look at all these people who've just got back from town. Someone could have used a public computer."

Lauren stared round at her fellow students. Some were taking off scarves and gloves and complaining about how cold it was outside. Allison was acting very chummy with Alfie, which made a change, Lauren thought, as she had spent most of last term throwing herself at Jay. Everyone looked so normal. And yet they could all be guilty.

Lauren narrowed her eyes. It could be anyone in the school, not just someone from this junior common room. She needed a plan!

She turned back to Katie, who had either forgotten about the stupid gossip already, or was putting on a brave face.

"Let's change the subject. Alfie's posting daily about his ghost research," Katie said. "He mentioned those two children, but then he says, 'the only other 'noteworthy' death at Amberwood was an old caretaker who died peacefully in his sleep while watching over the boiler in the cellar. I wonder if he's planning on taking his detector down there."

"Rather him than me." Lauren shuddered. She leaned over Katie's shoulder again to read the posts. Grace had told her that there was another ghost in the cellar. He never came out and kept very much to himself. Was that the old caretaker? She would have to warn Grace.

"Everyone's gone ghost mad!" Lauren murmured as she read. "Clothes going missing, noises in the night, doors closing on their own, sudden dips in temperature in certain rooms – is there anything they're not attributing to the paranormal?"

In a way, she was relieved. All the talk of ghosts took the sting out of the wicked whispers that the Secret Detective was spreading. And Alfie wasn't really going to discover Grace and Rodney, was he? But Grace was frightened, and Lauren owed it to her to protect her and Rodney. Anyway , they were *her* ghosts, and she didn't intend to share them with anyone else.

Alfie, alerted at the sound of his own name, came over with Allison shadowing him.

"Have you seen the response?" He grinned. "It's like having my own private network of ghost hunters. If it wasn't so cold today, I'd scan the grounds for the ghosts of those two children."

As if speaking about them had summoned them, Grace and Rodney melted through the common room walls and drifted over to Lauren. Even Lauren could barely see their shadowy forms. Were they trying to make themselves scarce, due to all the ghost searching?

They joined the group, leaning over Katie's shoulder. She shivered. "Has someone left the door open?"

Lauren looked pointedly at her spectral friends, but Rodney was already retreating. He was spinning round and round, up to the ceiling, laughing and crowing.

"I'm famous, Miss Lauren," he called. *"Have you seen what everyone's writing?"*

Then he took off like a tornado, swirling towards the curtains and making them billow.

Someone squealed. "What's happening?"

Alfie's face lit up. "There's something here," he breathed. "Talking about it must have summoned it. Darn it! Why did it have to manifest when I haven't got my detector on me?"

Lauren thought quickly and jumped up. She ran over to the window and nudged the catch before calling everyone's attention. "Look!" she cried. "The window wasn't shut properly. It's just the wind." She glared at Rodney. Grace was already doing her best to take him away.

Everyone went back to what they were doing, and Lauren returned to her group.

"That's why you were cold, Katie," she said. "It was nothing more than a draft."

"Well, that's your opinion," Alfie said, putting his hands on his hips and raising his voice. "I think it was ghosts, and I'm going to get my detector and check it out. Then I'm going to search the cellar." He looked round the room. "Anyone coming with me?"

Chapter Eleven

Immediately, half the students in the room clamoured round Alfie.

"I'll come!"

"I'll go with you as far as the door!"

"Just try and stop me!"

"Well, don't disappear," he ordered. "I'll race over to the dorm and get my detector. Back in a sec." And he sped away.

Grace flew close to Lauren. *"You need to go with them,"* she whispered.

Lauren nodded. She pretended to brush her hair out of her face. "I'm on it," she whispered back, behind her hand.

In the meantime, Ethan, who had only just finished rehearsal, and Jay, who had been doing special training with Mr Holt, came in demanding to know what all the excitement was about.

"We're going on a ghost hunt," Nyree informed them. "Alfie's gone to get his machine."

"Cool!" Ethan beamed. "Not outside though, I hope? I think it's beginning to snow!"

Nyree gave a small squeal and ran to the window. Sure enough, heavy flakes of snow were drifting down and settling on bushes and paths. She stared, mesmerised.

Lauren joined her. "It might not stay," she warned. "We often just get a squall like this, then it melts."

Nyree sighed. "I wish everywhere would be covered in white when we wake up tomorrow."

Lauren grinned and took her arm. "If it is," she said, "I'll teach you how to make the best snowballs. Come on. Alfie's back. Are you coming? Or do you want to stay here and watch the snow?"

Nyree turned reluctantly. "I'll come with you, of course," she stated. The fleeting excitement that had showed in her face at the snow disappeared back under her veil of indifference. Lauren gazed at her for a second or two, then went to join the others.

Five minutes later, a far larger group than was sensible followed Alfie into the corridor. With one hand, he held his EMF detector in front of him like a wand, while Allison clung to his free arm.

Lauren, her friends, and the two ghosts kept to the back. People who were trying to go in the opposite direction stared in surprise at the throng of juniors, whispering and giggling as they snaked along the corridors towards the entrance to the cellar. The door was under the back staircase, behind the kitchens.

Alfie shook Allison off and stretched out his hand to turn the handle. Lauren had a moment to wonder whether it would be locked, but it swung open without even a creak.

However, a loud bang sounded from the darkness beyond. Gasps and nervous giggles came from the group as they jostled each other and craned their necks to look down the forbidding stone staircase.

Lauren inclined her head at Rodney.

"Well, it's not me, is it?" he protested. *"I'm 'ere! Mebbe it's old Tom. He don't much like company."*

Alfie crept down the steps, one by one. Rodney, with a gleam in his eye, whizzed over everyone's heads and hovered above the detector. *"This'll scare 'em off,"* he chortled.

He pushed the air above the volume dial and suddenly all the lights flashed on and the device let out a heart-stopping screech.

The students who were closest to Alfie shrieked and ran back up the stairs. Allison was the first one out and she pushed past the ones still waiting, shaking her head. "I'm not going down there! And if you've all got any sense, you won't either." She loped away with more than half the group following. Even Alfie came back into the lighted corridor, his face paler than it had been a minute ago.

The remaining few exchanged glances. No one was game to continue. It was too scary! Lauren wanted to laugh. If only they knew! The ghosts were standing right beside them most of the time.

Alfie looked pleadingly at her, Katie, Nyree, Jay, and Ethan. "Will you come down with me?"

The boys agreed instantly.

"Of course, mate!" Jay said. "Let's do it!"

Lauren bit her lip. Rodney had just made things a hundred times worse. Instead of scaring Alfie away, he'd made him even more determined.

Keeping her promise to Grace, she sighed, "Okay, I'll come too." She pushed in front of the stragglers, who melted away.

Katie took her arm. "Let's get it over with!"

They tiptoed down into the cold, musty depths of the cellar. Nyree was directly behind them, and Jay and Ethan brought up the rear. Grace and Rodney swooped ahead.

Lauren found a light switch and snapped it on. But it only lit a single bare bulb hanging down from the centre of the cavernous room. The weak light barely reached the corners and darkness spilled out of open doors leading to smaller rooms.

Lauren shivered as she peered into the gloom. It was so cold down here! She stared at the bizarre mixture of old and new. At intervals around three walls were arched alcoves full of old pieces of stage scenery and broken barres; in one cleared out corner, the students' suitcases and trunks were piled high. Lauren picked out her own rather shabby cases stacked next to Katie's posh ones.

Then, amongst the chaos and looking totally out of character, the fourth wall glowed with lights from modern glass-fronted cabinets housing the cables, hubs and routers for the school's wi-fi system.

And, in front of the remnants of an old boiler that had been cleared to make way for the pipes, levers and cables of a modern heating system, sat the ghost of an old caretaker, glowering at the invasion of students into his domain. He pushed back his flat cap and wiped his hands on his dirty grey overalls. Then he balled his fists as though he was preparing for a fight. He met Lauren's nervous gaze with a scowl.

Lauren gulped and took a step back.

"Don't be alarmed," Grace whispered by her side. *"Old Tom only looks fierce. He's a big softy, really."*

Alfie aimed his detector at the pile of rubble that had once been a boiler. The machine started to hum and Alfie's hand shook with excitement. Lauren felt her heart miss a beat. Was the machine really working?

But Rodney, looking like he was about to explode with mischief, was hovering with his hand over the dial. Lauren frowned. She had to stop him! Only, apart from knocking the detector out of Alfie's hand, she was out of ideas. She was still hesitating when suddenly Old Tom bellowed, *"Turn that confounded racket off!"*

Instantly, the grin left Rodney's face and he turned the dial on the detector. The noise stopped abruptly, and Rodney doffed his cap at the old ghost.

Alfie shook the machine and put it to his ear. "Rats," he snarled. "Either it's stopped working or the spirits have gone."

"Or they were never here in the first place," Lauren said firmly. "Maybe it was picking up the electrical cables?"

"Oh, they were here all right!" Alfie beamed. He continued to inspect his device, unaware that Rodney was floating beside him with his hand sunk into the plastic.

"Maybe it needs new batteries," Alfie muttered, turning the device one way and another while Rodney pretended to writhe in pain.

Lauren glared at the playful ghost. It was all a game to him, but couldn't he see he was freaking Grace out? Not to mention encouraging Alfie to go further with his hunt for the ghosts. It could have awful consequences for them. She was about to suggest they leave when a noise from behind them made everyone jump.

"What was that?" Katie whispered, her voice shaking.

"Something by the stairs," Ethan murmured, moving closer to her.

They all looked intently at the staircase, which was in the shadows. Then footsteps sounded on the stone, slow, heavy, and deliberate. Lauren felt the hairs on the back of her neck stand on end. She shook herself. She was being silly. She knew the ghosts!

"There's nothing to be afraid of," she forced herself to utter while her heart pounded.

"That depends on how much you fear your headmistress," came the stern voice of Mrs Herriott from the darkness at the bottom of the stairs. Then she moved forward into the centre of the room, where the meagre light was strongest.

"I've never heard such a hullabaloo in my life," she scolded, her arms folded firmly across her chest. "Students running through the corridors, screaming their heads off about ghosts in the cellar. Whatever next?"

Lauren looked at her feet. She could feel the blood rising in her cheeks. Luckily it was dark and no one else could see it! The others shifted in embarrassment, and Lauren spotted Alfie slipping the detector into his hoodie pocket.

"Catherine? I'm surprised at you," Mrs Herriott snapped. "I had you down for a sensible one. As for you, Alfie McCarthy, I know you're the ringleader in all this ghost nonsense. Go back to your common room and don't let me catch you down here ever again."

"Sorry, Mrs Herriott," Alfie mumbled.

"I've a good mind to ban you all from the Valentine's dance," Mrs Herriott continued. Everyone gasped. "But that wouldn't be fair to the local school who are putting in so much effort." She tapped her foot on the floor. "So, you can each write a 500-word essay on the life of Anna Pavlova. This evening. Instead of Sunday film night."

She turned back to the stairs. "I want those essays on my desk before bedtime." And she left.

The friends looked at each other and tried to smile.

"It could have been worse," Alfie said as they headed for the stairs too. "She could have confiscated my detector!"

Chapter Twelve

On the morning of the Valentine's Party, Grace hovered in the hall of the main house. She had intended to watch the seniors in their *pas de deux* class with Miss Radcliffe, but she felt too agitated. Alfie, far from being discouraged, was continuing to stir up the other students about ghost-hunting, and she didn't like the way things were building up.

Lauren had assured her that his device was a waste of money and couldn't possibly work, but Rodney's antics in the cellar had made Alfie believe it did. And now there was no stopping the curious boy. He hadn't ventured into the cellar again, and snow had kept everyone huddled around the radiators indoors, so he hadn't tried waving his silly machine around in the grounds, but Grace was afraid it was only a matter of time. She twirled her fingers in her ringlets while she thought. She knew that all she had to do was keep out of Alfie's way, but that wasn't always possible.

Like now! There he was, strolling along with Allison hanging on to his every word. Grace pulled into the shadows to watch them.

"Who from?" Allison was saying.

"Someone called Piper Lapiz," Alfie replied, as they passed Grace's hiding place. "She's a newspaper journalist. I got the email this morning. She's seen some of my posts on

The Paranormal Society page and she wants to interview me about Amberwood. She's going to come to the school and get Mrs Herriott's permission. Isn't it awesome? Someone out there is actually taking me seriously."

Grace gasped. This was getting worse and worse! A journalist? Where would it end? With an actual professional ghost hunter?

Allison pulled a face. "Do you think Mrs H will agree? She was so angry about the cellar business."

Alfie shrugged. "Hopefully she'll welcome the publicity for the school," he declared. "After all, it's a big newspaper, not just a local rag."

"When's she coming?"

"I don't know. She didn't give me a date."

"Well, I can help you in the interview, if you like," Allison said, flicking her hair behind her shoulder. "Do you think she'll want to take photos?" she simpered.

They turned the corner towards the canteen and Grace floated away in the opposite direction, frowning. The world didn't need to start poking around to find ghosts at Amberwood. She and Rodney had always been so careful, and up to now, only Lauren knew of their existence. And *she* had been unwavering in her loyalty, not even telling her best friend, Katie.

Grace tortured herself with a mental image of wild-eyed characters hiding in the bushes, brandishing cameras or detectors (some of which might actually work!), trying to catch images of her and Rodney.

She was so lost in her thoughts that she didn't see the two matrons coming towards her till it was too late and the deputy, Mrs Rowland, passed through Grace's form with an exaggerated shiver.

"Are you cold?" Matron asked.

"I just felt like I walked through a fridge." Mrs Rowland laughed. "It must be because you were going to tell me about those dowsing rods." She gestured to two steel rods, shaped like an L, in Matron's hand.

Grace stared at them in fascination as well. Weren't they for discovering underground water?

Matron scratched her nose with her free hand. "Mr. Grant confiscated them off Alfie," she said. "Apparently David had gone to the library early for young Nyree's private maths lesson, and he found Alfie walking up and down with these. He was insisting to Nyree that they could detect ghosts."

"Why was Alfie in the library? Shouldn't he have been in a lesson of his own? I hope he wasn't scaring the poor girl." Mrs Rowland frowned.

Matron chuckled. "According to David, she was just staring at Alfie as if he was two years younger than her, rather than the other way about. But David confiscated them anyway. There's quite a collection of ghost hunting implements in my office now. I'm forever falling over feathers, thermometers and chalk circles. The entire school has gone ghost mad."

Grace rolled her eyes. Rodney had so much to answer for!

Mrs Rowland shivered again and Grace drew a bit further away. She was about to whizz off and look for Rodney, but Mrs Rowland's next comment made her pause.

"You know, I'm not sure if there isn't something in all this ghost talk, after all."

Matron raised her eyebrows at the younger woman.

"It's just that," Mrs Rowland continued hesitantly, "last Saturday morning, I couldn't find my house keys. I searched high and low and in the end was going to ask you for yours, to get some more cut. Then, on Saturday evening, there they were! Exactly where they should have been and where I'd looked a hundred times. Isn't that the sort of trick they say poltergeists play?"

Grace's hand flew to her mouth. Just wait till she got hold of Rodney. It was time he went on one of his famous jaunts and let things at Amberwood simmer down.

Matron, however, was laughing. "You're working too hard, Jen," she comforted. "This is a school! Things are always disappearing and reappearing. Kids move things, forget where they've put things, pick things up that don't belong to them, then put them down elsewhere."

"I suppose so," Mrs Rowland murmured. She shook herself. "Well, it wouldn't do for me to add fuel to the rumours!"

Grace had heard enough. She swooped away in search of Rodney. She would persuade him to go on a visit to one of his precious racecourses. It wasn't like him to stick around at Amberwood for so long anyway.

After searching Rodney's favourite haunts, Grace found the mischievous stable boy in the computer room. He was diving in and out of the monitors. Three students were trying to use them, and Rodney was driving them crazy with frustration. Grace couldn't blame him really: it was something she'd done in the past. But it was more serious now, and he had to stop.

"*Rodney*!" she called.

Rodney pulled up short and doffed his cap at her while splitting his face with a huge grin. The students stood up and grumbled that someone really needed to do something about the wi-Fi in this school. They gathered their belongings and left.

Grace told Rodney what she'd heard Alfie telling Allison. "*We could be in real danger if professional people start poking around looking for us*," she finished.

"*Aw, hang it all, yer Grace*," Rodney cajoled. "*I can escape any ghost-routing cove in a twinkling. Just let them try and exercise me!*"

"It's ex-or-cise, remember?" Grace smiled despite her worries. *"But that's not the point, Rodney. I know we can go away till things calm down if we need to, but I don't want my home turned into a circus. All I've ever wanted is for it to be a renowned ballet school, not a notorious haunted house."*

Rodney scuffed the skirting boards with his toes. *"All right, yer Grace. I'll tone things down. Let the heat go down."* He looked at her from under the brim of his cap. *"But there really ain't nothing to be afraid of. That machine's nonsense and Alfie's just a curious lad. He's no danger."*

They both whirled round at the sound of the door. Grace's face softened when she saw it was Katie. The ghosts watched her settle herself at a computer and switch it on. Instantly, she was engrossed in her work.

A gleam came into Rodney's eye and he pulled himself up tall.

"Oh, no, you don't!" Grace warned. And he wilted.

"Dash it all," he grumbled. *"I shall visit old Lord Chesholme."*

And he vanished.

Grace was about to withdraw as well when suddenly she heard Katie gasp. Grace glanced at her and saw with a shock how white Katie's face had gone under her shiny auburn hair. Then tears appeared in the corners of her soft grey eyes.

Grace swooped over to the monitor to see what Katie was reading. Her hand flew to her mouth. It was another wicked comment from the Secret Detective, as Nyree had christened the rumourmonger.

The tears trickled down Katie's cheeks. Grace didn't waste another moment. She rushed out and flew through the school, looking for Lauren.

She found her and Nyree in the dormitory, choosing clothes for the Valentine's party that evening. Grace heard Nyree ask Lauren whether Mrs Herriott would even allow her to go.

"By rights, I should," Nyree was saying, "because I am in Year Nine. But I'm afraid Mrs Herriott will say it doesn't count because I'm only eleven."

"Well, she hasn't said you can't, has she?" Lauren offered. "Just get on the bus with the rest of us and see what happens."

Nyree turned as Grace approached and Grace stiffened. But Nyree's eyes looked straight through her to the wall beyond, so Grace relaxed and went up to Lauren.

"You need to go to the computer room," she murmured. Lauren stilled. She inclined her head, as though trying to

choose between leggings. *"It's Katie,"* Grace continued. *"She needs you. Right now!"*

Lauren shoved her selection of clothes back in the drawer and slammed it shut. She turned to Nyree. "I've just remembered," she said. "I need to ask Katie something. Why don't you go ahead to class, and I'll meet you there?"

Nyree shoved her hands into her pockets. "I prefer to go with you," she said in a low voice.

"Go, Lauren," Grace urged. *"There's no time for arguments."*

Lauren held up her hands. "Come on, then!"

The two girls hurried to the computer room, with Grace leading the way.

When they got there, it was empty. Katie had already gone. But she'd left the computer switched on. Grace floated in front of the screen and gestured to Lauren to come and look.

Lauren and Nyree stared at the message with the avatar of the Secret Detective. It was short, and it said:

"L and E,
Sitting in a tree,
K-I-S-S-I-N-G..."

Chapter Thirteen

Swallowing an ache in her throat, Lauren sped out of the computer room, forgetting about Nyree, who could barely keep up. Lauren ran like the wind across the school grounds to the stable block. She wanted to speak to Katie before class. She needed to clear up this stupid rumour once and for all.

Katie was already in the studio, warming up. Her mouth was a straight line. Her usual peaches and cream complexion was chalky white. Lauren strode over to her.

"Katie, I've seen it," she started without preamble.

"I think everyone has," Katie snarled.

"But you don't believe it, do you?" Lauren hissed. She glanced round at the other students. The ones standing nearest had stopped talking suddenly. "It's just a stupid childish rhyme. Ethan and I haven't been kissing in a tree, or anywhere!"

"I know it's not literal, Lauren," Katie snapped. She bent down to adjust her ribbons, but not before Lauren saw her cheeks were flaming.

Lauren looked round in desperation. Where was Ethan to back her up? He was laughing and joking with Jay, Alfie and Mark on the other side of the room. Lauren tried to catch his eye and call him over, but at that moment, Mr Holt came in and there was no more time for chatting.

Lauren tried to concentrate on her barre work. But she kept going over things in her head. Who would want to do this? What did they have to gain? She studied the classmates she could see, suspecting each and every one of them.

Every time they changed sides, she tried to catch Katie's eye. But Katie ignored her. Lauren gritted her teeth. Her mind spun with all the things she wanted to say to this evil Secret Detective. She was so tense she could barely move her foot in the tiny beats that were needed for *petits battements*.

"Relax, Lauren," Mr Holt murmured as he walked along the line of students. He jiggled Lauren's hand to loosen it up. She took a deep breath and tried to do as he asked.

Maybe she should talk to Ethan about it, she thought, as everyone marked the free *enchaînements* in the centre. But he must have seen the messages, too. Hadn't he tried to put Katie's mind at rest?

"Lauren!" Mr Holt chided. "You're going the wrong way!"

Lauren came back to earth with a bump and stared into Allison's livid face as they were about to collide. Hastily, she turned to the other side and tried to remember which step came next.

"Some of us need to concentrate on the job at hand, not on tonight's Valentine's party," Mr Holt said, but with a twinkle in his eye. He gestured for the *reverence*.

As soon as the last note faded away, Lauren grabbed her things and caught up with Katie in the changing room.

"Katie, please," she begged. "Don't believe this rubbish. You know I would never do anything to hurt you! Ethan and I do get together in the breaks during rehearsal because we always hang around in the same group. He's not going to go and chat with Allison, is he? It's all perfectly boring and innocent."

Katie's face softened. She picked at the school badge on her sweatshirt. "I didn't want to believe it," she murmured. "But it was a bit of a shock. And everyone's saying there's no smoke without fire, so that doesn't help. But," she squeezed Lauren's hand, "let's forget it, shall we? And spend more time trying to catch this person out. This totally isn’t what I wanted the Gossip Wall to be used for! The magazine committee is already saying that if the poisonous messages don’t stop, they’ll take down the Wall."

Lauren breathed a sigh of relief. Then she had an idea. "Maybe Mark could trace the computer that's being used. Isn't that what they do in films? Someone always knows how to do it, and Mark is pretty switched on with IT," she suggested.

"It's worth a shot, I guess," Katie agreed.

Lauren nodded. "I'll wait for him. You go on ahead."

Katie picked up her kit and suggested to Nyree that they get a drink, then check on their outfits for the party.

Lauren hung back at the bottom of the stairs to the boys' dormitory, waiting for them to come down. There had been classes in all four studios this afternoon, so the building was busy. Some boys had already gone. Lauren always suspected they didn't bother showering after class! But after a while, Jay and Ethan appeared.

Lauren took the opportunity to get Ethan's support. She grabbed his arm. "Can I have a word? Just the two of us," she said, with a pointed look at Jay.

Jay raised his eyebrows, then he shrugged and walked away.

"Have you seen this latest stupid post?" Lauren asked as soon as Jay was out of hearing.

"What post?" Ethan was clearly in the dark, so Lauren filled him in.

"It's just horrible," Lauren finished, "and I don't think Katie's buying my explanations. You've got to tell her there's nothing going on between us, Ethan."

Ethan rolled his eyes and scuffed the bottom stair with his toe. "You know what?" he said. "You're both making a big deal over nothing. It's just spiteful lies. Why take any notice? I don't even bother reading the Gossip Wall anymore." He shifted his kit bag to the other shoulder. "And I hate it that everyone's going on as if Katie and I are engaged!" he finished. "We're only thirteen! We're just friends."

Lauren's mouth fell open. She didn't know what to say. More boys clattered down the stairs, and Ethan gave her a quick nod before joining them to go to the main house.

Lauren hung around for a while, but Mark didn't appear. He must have already left, she thought. She would catch him in the common room.

Her fingers wrapped around her mobile in her pocket. Or, what about asking Mum to ask Nick if he knew a way she could find this person's computer? It was a thought. She took out her mobile and switched it on.

It opened at the *En Pointe* Gossip Wall page, where she had left it last time. Instantly she saw the dreaded avatar heading a new post:

"Some people aren't satisfied with being the best dancers in the school. They have to steal other people's boyfriends too."

There were no names, but coming so close to the last one, it was clear who the Secret Detective meant.

Lauren gritted her teeth. Well, she could take it. She knew it wasn't true. As long as Katie continued to believe her too, that was all that mattered.

Lauren pressed the key for 'Mum' and almost cried with relief when her mum answered on the second ring.

"Hello poppet, I wasn't expecting to hear from you today. Haven't you got that party on at the local school?"

"Yes, but not till later. I wanted to say hi," Lauren started.

"That's lovely!" Mum said. "I was just about to text you. Nick and I are at this fabulous hotel in the Lake District. There's a do on tonight too – dinner and dancing. You should see the dining room! It's all red velvet, bows and hearts, and totally shimmers with all the crystal glasses under the lights. I've never seen anything so romantic! I'll WhatsApp you some photos."

"You didn't tell me you were going away!" Lauren said in a small voice.

"It was a surprise." Mum chuckled. "I didn't know myself till this afternoon. Did you want something in particular, or were you just calling for a quick chat?"

Lauren took a deep breath. How could she tell Mum about what was going on now? It would spoil her weekend if she thought Lauren was having problems.

"No," she managed. "Nothing special. You have a great time!"

"Thanks, my love! Oops, gotta go! We're having a champagne tea as dinner isn't till quite late."

"Have a great time," Lauren said and she pressed end.

Then she squared her shoulders and picked up her bag. She would just have to sort things out on her own.

Anyway, it was time to get ready for the party. She wasn't going to let any stupid Secret Detective spoil tonight.

Chapter Fourteen

Although it was only five o'clock, it was already dark when the Years Nine and Ten piled onto the coach that was taking them to the local school for the Valentine's dance.

Lauren shivered in her Lycra pants and off the shoulder top even though it had long flared sleeves. She was glad she was wearing trainers and not skimpy little evening sandals like Allison, who was trying unsuccessfully to avoid puddles.

Katie had plaited her auburn hair the previous night, then brushed it out so that it fell in soft waves around her face. Lauren decided she looked like a modern Alice in Wonderland with her blue chiffon dress that reminded Lauren of Grace.

Thinking of which... she looked around, but the ghosts were nowhere to be seen.

Lauren and Nyree sat in seats in the middle of the coach. Ethan and Katie sat in the two in front of them and Jay and Mark behind. Alfie had joined Allison and her gang along the back seat, but they had just got settled when five Year Tens ordered them to find somewhere else.

Ethan turned round and grinned at Nyree. "They let you come, then?"

She looked at him solemnly and put her finger to her lips. "Shh. We haven't left yet. No one has 'let me come'. But no one has said I can't come. Don't attract attention." She sent a dark look to Miss Radcliffe, who was sitting in the front, chatting to the driver.

Ethan nodded and turned back to talk to Katie.

Lauren checked her mascara in a tiny mirror that she had in her shoulder bag. She would have liked to sit with Katie. Or even Jay. But somehow she was with Nyree yet again. That girl just wouldn't leave her alone. Lauren glanced at her sideways. What if she was the Secret Detective? Then she shook herself and looked out of the window, dismissing the tiny niggle that had wormed its way into her brain.

Suddenly, Nyree's hand gripped her thigh.

"Wha...? Oh!" Lauren saw Mrs Herriott pulling herself up the coach steps and begin to count heads. Nyree's fingers dug deeper and deeper into Lauren's flesh as the headmistress got closer. They could hear her counting under her breath, "Twenty-seven, twenty-eight, twenty-nine," then she passed by.

Three rows from the back, she stopped, turned round and went back to the front of the coach.

"Listen up, everybody," she called. Instantly there was silence and thirty-four pairs of eyes locked onto the Head. "I want you all to have a wonderful time. But I want you to remember that you are ambassadors for Amberwood Hall and if I hear of any bad behaviour, any drinking of things that are not provided by the school or slipping off to places where you can't be found, there will be dire consequences."

Nobody spoke.

"If you wish to remain a student at Amberwood, you'll think about my words before doing anything that could jeopardise that."

There was an indistinct murmur interspersed with, "Yes, Mrs Herriott," and the headmistress smiled. "Miss Radcliffe is accompanying you there and back on the coach, but teachers from Marshwood will supervise once you get there." Then she walked directly towards Lauren and Nyree. Lauren thought the girl's fingers would reach bone if she squeezed Lauren's leg any harder. She was about to prise her hand off when Mrs Herriott spoke. "Nyree, if you feel uncomfortable and want to come back to school, get Lauren to phone Mrs Rowland and she'll come and pick you up, all right?"

Nyree just stared at her, so Lauren answered. "We will, Mrs Herriott, thank you!" and Mrs Herriott left the bus with a wave.

"Thanks for the bruises," Lauren complained as Nyree's grip relaxed and the coach pulled away from the school.

"You're welcome!" Nyree replied calmly.

Lauren gave up and stared into the darkness beyond the window again.

It only took twenty minutes to get to Marshwood, the town's secondary school, and soon everyone was piling into the lobby and exclaiming in delight. Two rows of red and white heart-shaped bunting formed a corridor which led them to the main hall.

Just inside was a cardboard photo booth and a Year Ten boy was waving a digital camera.

"Come and get your photo taken before you get stuck in," he called. "There's all sorts of things to dress up in."

Lauren, Katie, Jay, Ethan, Mark and Nyree piled into the flimsy booth and shouted with laughter as Ethan stuck a false moustache under his nose and struck a dramatic pose. Katie and Lauren pulled feather boas around their shoulders and Jay slapped a Stetson hat onto his head. Nyree found a cat mask and stared at the camera from behind it. Mark swept a vampire type cloak around his shoulders and bared his teeth. The fun had begun!

Once the photographer was satisfied that he'd got them all, they scrambled out and went into the huge assembly hall.

Katie gasped. "WOWZER! They must have an amazing art department!"

Hundreds of cut-out hearts hung from the ceiling. They were attached with clear twine, which made it look like they were floating in the air. Chairs and tables, covered in pink crepe paper tied with gigantic white crepe paper bows, lined the hall, creating an area for dancing in the middle.

On the two back corners of a long buffet table floated bouquets of helium balloons, silver, red and white, which sparkled in the rotating lights.

"Food!" cried Jay, his eyes widening. He made a beeline for the laden table.

The others followed to admire the pink and white cupcakes, biscuits and lollipops shaped like hearts and even strawberries cut into heart shapes and interspersed on a skewer with grapes. There were also healthy salads and cheeses, sausage rolls and chicken drumsticks. Jay's hand was reaching out for an enormous rose-shaped cookie when an excited squeal stopped him short.

Out of nowhere came Lizzie, dazzling in a blue, white and red sequined mini skirt and silver tank top.

"You're here! I can't believe it!" she shouted as she threw her arms around Lauren and Katie. "And who's the Year Seven?" she asked as she saw Nyree behind Lauren. "The school mascot?"

"I'm not a Year Seven or a mascot," retorted Nyree. "I'm in Year Nine, though I expect I'll be in Year Ten next term."

Everyone laughed at Lizzie's look of confusion. Lauren took her arm. "I'll explain," she said, "but first of all, I LOVE your outfit. It's so wild!"

Lizzie shook her brown curly hair, which was longer and frizzier than Lauren remembered. "It's gotta be done!" she laughed. "Come and help me start the dancing. No one's got the guts to be first!"

Katie looked at Ethan. "Shall we?" She grinned. He grabbed her hand, and they ran to the centre of the room, which was empty.

Jay abandoned his mission to fill his stomach and held his hand out to Lauren. "Shall *we*?"

Lauren couldn't wait to dance! "Are you supposed to?" she said.

"I'll be fine," Jay assured her. "I'll only have one dance and I won't go mad."

"I'll just watch," said Nyree.

Once the Amberwood students set the ball rolling, the floor was soon full of boys and girls from both schools, swaying and stepping, gyrating and twirling.

After a while, Jay shouted to Lauren. "It's getting a bit wild! I'm going to get something to eat."

She nodded. Jay slipped away to the buffet table and instantly a local Year Ten boy took his place, dancing opposite Lauren to the latest Post Malone track.

Lauren took a moment to check for Nyree. She was sucking on a heart-shaped lollipop, wandering around the gyrating crowd, drinking in the atmosphere. She gave Lauren a thumbs-up and tilted her head in an approving way towards Lauren's new partner.

The music was thunderous! It was impossible to talk, so Lauren threw herself into dancing. Everyone was laughing and trying to outdo everyone else with inventive moves.

Lauren glanced over at Ethan. He was the king of this type of dancing, and it was no wonder he was in the centre of a throng of admirers.

Suddenly, Lizzie grabbed Lauren's arm. "Get ready," she yelled. And the hall filled with the track that they had done their YouTube choreography to last year. Instantly, the team fell into place and picked up the beat. Lauren felt another body squeeze in and turned in time to see Ethan take up centre place. She stepped to the side to give him room, but he fell in behind her and grabbed her waist. Then he put his mouth against her ear and whispered, "Cartwheel!"

Lauren caught on immediately. She stood with her arms and legs wide, holding her body rigid so that Ethan could flip her over in a cartwheel in front of him. Her hands didn't touch the ground. Her hair stuck to her face as she came upright again, and they twirled and leaped together. They adapted the moves from the choreography as though they'd rehearsed it thousands of times.

Eventually the track ended, and Lauren gasped for breath through her smiles. She and Ethan took a mock bow, then Ethan pulled her arm up with his, the way athletes do on a podium.

Lauren laughed as the audience erupted in applause. But suddenly, across the room, she caught Katie's eye.

Katie was staring at Lauren in dismay.

Chapter Fifteen

On the journey back to Amberwood, while Nyree slept on the seat next to her, Lauren picked at her cuticles. She hadn't felt this lonely since her first week at Amberwood. And even then, she and Katie had become friends almost immediately.

Every so often she darted a glance towards her best friend and Ethan, who were sitting together but could have been at different ends of the coach thanks to the icy atmosphere between them. Jay, Mark, and Alfie were talking about sports and taking no notice of anyone else. Allison kept sending knowing looks Lauren's way while she whispered and giggled with her gang behind their hands.

Lauren shifted in her seat. She didn't want to look at them, but she could still see their reflections in the dark window. What could they be gossiping about? she thought crossly. She hadn't done anything wrong. It wasn't a crime to dance with a classmate, was it?

Maybe one of them was the Secret Detective? She wouldn't put anything past Allison! But what did she have to gain? Did she just dislike Lauren that much?

Or maybe it was Emily or Nicola, wanting to make a good impression on Allison. They seemed to hero-worship her after all.

Lauren looked down at her fingernails, trying to appear totally cool. In reality she was curling up inside. It was a very lonely place when you suspected everyone around you. She battled with her thoughts till they arrived back at Amberwood and she shook Nyree a little harder than she had intended.

"We're here," she said, and she stood up and strode to the front of the coach so she was first off. She couldn't bear the way everyone was looking at her.

There was no sign of Katie when Lauren went up to the dorm. But she must have slipped in soon after because by the time Lauren got back from the bathroom, Katie was already in bed, curled into a ball with her eyes tight shut.

Lauren got into her own bed and squeezed her hands into fists. Should she try to talk to Katie? She couldn't really be asleep! No one fell asleep that quickly. Lauren stared at the motionless lump in Katie's bed. The message was loud and clear that Katie wasn't in the mood to talk.

Lauren turned over. Maybe she should wait till everyone was asleep, then find Grace. Didn't the ghost often spend the nights in the attic studio? At least Lauren could get to talk to her spectral friend on her own.

But while she was planning her midnight escapade, Lauren fell into a deep sleep and didn't stir till the bell went next morning.

Throughout breakfast, Lauren avoided eye contact with her fellow students. They were all pouring over their phones and when Lauren switched hers on, she saw another mean post from the Secret Detective:

"So, L and E decided to go public! What a performance!"

Lauren gritted her teeth. The Secret Detective had just made her, or his, first mistake. If she, or he, knew about her dance with Ethan, that meant it had to be someone from Year Nine or Ten.

Maybe she could catch them now! She wracked her brains for a way to get rid of Nyree for half an hour so she could find Grace and get her help. An idea came to her when she heard Allison asking Emily to get her some washing powder if she was going into town that morning.

"But it's Sunday," Emily protested.

"Well, you'll just have to let me have some of yours, then," Allison retorted, and Lauren formed her plan. She was ready, as soon as Nyree asked her daily question of, "what do we do now?"

"You need to wash your kit for next week," Lauren said firmly.

"But I washed my leotard and tights yesterday," Nyree argued.

"No, I mean everything. Leg-warmers, crossover, the lot."

Nyree brightened. "Okay. Are you coming with me?"

"No. I have something I need to do, so you start and I'll come and find you in a minute."

Nyree's shoulders sagged. "I'll come with you, and we'll do our washing afterward," she insisted.

Lauren gave her a little push. "Just go, Nyree. I won't be long."

With dragging feet and her head down, Nyree left for the dormitory.

As soon as she was out of sight, Lauren sprinted to the back stairs and bounded up to the attic studio. There was no guarantee Grace would be there, but it was the most likely place.

She was in luck and almost burst into tears of relief when she saw the ghost dancing in the dust motes that floated in the air.

"Hello, Lauren! How was the party?" Grace's face lit up with a huge welcoming smile and, once again, Lauren found herself wishing she could hug her.

"Mixed," Lauren said in a small voice, and threw herself onto the floor in the middle of the room. "I thought you'd be there."

"I know," Grace said sadly. "I would have adored it! I feel like I'm missing out on all the fun. But Rodney has gone off on a jaunt and I decided it would be too risky. There may have been someone there who could see me, and I didn't want to give Alfie any more ammunition." She squared her shoulders and smiled at Lauren. "I'm sure all this ghost hunting nonsense will die down soon. In the meantime, tell me about the party!"

Lauren, hoping Grace was right, told her how everything had been wonderful to start with. Then it had all turned to worms. She showed her the recent posts from the Secret Detective.

"Katie isn't speaking to me," she finished miserably as she put the phone away. She took a deep breath. "I really need your help, Grace!"

"Anything!" the ghost promised.

"Could you and Rodney keep watch on all the school computers and check on what people are doing on them?"

Grace frowned. "Rodney hasn't come back yet and I can't be everywhere at once, Lauren! There are computers in the IT room, one in the library, in the staff room, in the admin office, in Mrs Herriott's office. Not to mention all the personal laptops and mobile phones." She floated away with her finger pressed to her temple like she was trying to find a solution.

"I know, but we have to start somewhere," Lauren insisted. "I need to prove to Katie that it's all lies. I don't want to lose my best friend. And that's what's happening." She nibbled on her bottom lip as she watched Grace drifting gently in the dust.

"Actually," Lauren said. "You probably only need to monitor the computer in the library."

"Oh?"

Lauren drew a circle in the dust with her forefinger. She didn't look up at Grace. "That's where Nyree does her private maths lessons. She'd have loads of time to be the Secret Detective."

Grace whirled round. "Nyree?" she cried. "Lauren, you can't possibly think it's Nyree. She adores you! Why would she make hurtful comments about you?"

Lauren shifted uncomfortably. "Well, she's the only person I can think of with anything to gain," she said. "She could be doing it to break up my friendship with Katie. So that she has me all to herself."

Grace frowned. "I can't see it," she said. "But I'll watch her if that's what you want. I said I'd do anything."

"Thanks," Lauren muttered. But she didn't feel the relief she had thought she would. Was Grace cross with her, too? She stood up and stretched. "I'd better go. See you later?"

Grace nodded and Lauren ran back downstairs towards the common room, feeling slightly guilty that she wasn't joining Nyree as she'd promised.

As she walked through the corridors, Lauren's cheeks burned. Was it her imagination, or did people stop talking when she went past? And did they turn their backs on purpose? She lowered her head and sighed with relief when she got to the common room door.

Again, the hum of conversation stopped when Lauren entered. A crowd of girls had gathered round Katie, who was sitting at the central table with her laptop open. Her face was like stone and she was staring at the screen while others pointed and whispered. Lauren noticed that none of the boys were there.

She strode across and the others melted away.

"What's happened now?" she demanded.

Katie gestured to the screen where the dreaded avatar of the Secret Detective took up most of the page. Alongside was the message:

"I overheard L talking to E about K: "You've got to tell her!"
Tell her what? That you're with L now?"

Lauren thought she would explode. That was totally out of context! And it was days ago: that time after class when she'd been asking Ethan to help her prove to Katie that nothing was going on between them.

Lauren put her hand on the laptop lid to close it, then froze. On the other hand, it meant that the Secret Detective had to be someone who was in the stable block at that time. There hadn't been anyone in the corridor as far as she remembered, but what classes had been going on? Who could have been lurking behind a door or round a corner?

She slammed the lid down, and Katie recoiled. Lauren turned her chair round and looked her in the eyes. "Katie, can't you see that this is ridiculous? This horrible person has twisted my meaning by leaving half the conversation out. I was telling Ethan that he needs to tell you how much this is all nonsense."

Katie raised her grey eyes to Lauren. "Ah, but he hasn't," she whispered.

"We've talked about this. Please take no notice," Lauren begged, her eyes filling with tears.

Katie held up her palms. "People are right. Is there ever smoke without fire? I mean, the Secret Detective seems to be finding an awful lot to comment on."

Lauren stared at her in dismay. "I swear I'll find out who's doing it."

Katie's jaw tightened. "Well, you haven't got much time. Hannah is losing patience and wants to close the page down."

"Don't let her do that," Lauren pleaded. "I'll have no chance of catching her," she caught herself just in time, "or him, if it closes down."

Katie narrowed her eyes and shrugged. She gathered up her laptop and moved away.

Lauren stared in dismay at her friend's retreating back.

At that moment, the door opened and Nyree came in. She made a beeline for Lauren.

"Where have you been?" Lauren snapped.

"Washing my kit like you told me," Nyree reminded her, looking mildly surprised. "Don't forget all the Houses have got rehearsal in half an hour. Don't you think we should get ready?"

Lauren had forgotten. She took one last look at the back of Katie's head and went off to get her kit bag.

The stable block was noisy and crowded. All four Houses were rehearsing so every studio was full.

Lauren and Nyree slipped into Studio Two, where Helena was about to run through a warm-up for Spartacus House.

"Nyree!" Julian called. "Why are you wearing netball kit? And why aren't you wearing shoes?"

Nyree looked down at her brown toes, curling slightly on the cold floorboards. "My shoes are wet," she said. "I'm wearing my feet."

Everyone laughed, but Lauren couldn't even break a smile. She felt so wretched. Fleetingly, she realised she shouldn't have told Nyree to wash ALL her kit.

Rehearsal got under way but for the first time, not even dancing made Lauren feel better. She wasn't finding her part challenging enough. The steps that Julian had set for her to do, while attached to puppet strings that he was controlling from a box above her, were very simple. She was restricted to the small space in front of the box and wasn't even dancing en pointe. A Year Seven could have done it. She was relieved when Julian called a halt for the day. She was even more relieved when he asked Nyree to stay for another half hour to go over her part.

Lauren didn't speak to anyone while she was changing. She stuffed her used kit into her bag then, on a whim, she dragged everything out of her locker and threw it all in too. She would take her own advice to Nyree and do a mammoth wash, shoes and all! Heaving the now stuffed kit bag onto her shoulder, she slipped out and began to trudge back to the main house.

She didn't look round when she heard footsteps running to catch her up. It couldn't be Nyree! Half an hour hadn't gone by yet, and then she would have to change.

But it was Ethan. "You look whacked," he said with concern. "And that kit bag looks like it weighs a ton. Here, let me take it for you."

Lauren looked around uneasily. Was anyone watching? Ready to report maliciously on another innocent encounter?

Feeling guilty for being anywhere near Ethan, she turned away. "It's OK," she said. "You go on."

Ethan grabbed her arm and turned her back to face him. "Lauren, don't let these stupid rumours make you paranoid. They're all nonsense. We know that. We should just ignore them."

"But can't you see how much the gossip is hurting Katie, Ethan? She's my best friend and she doesn't even want to talk to me!"

Ethan sighed. "I know. And that sucks. But it's a small school, Lauren. We can't avoid each other. We'll just have to prove to Katie that there's nothing suspicious going on by acting normally and soon everyone will get bored. We've got nothing to hide! Here," he stretched out his hand, "let me take your bag."

Reluctantly, Lauren handed over the bag.

Ethan pretended to stagger under the weight. "Are you running away?" he teased. "Or have you got a body in here and I've just prevented you from sneaking into the woods to bury it?"

"Just having a clear out," Lauren admitted.

Ethan continued to act the fool and make jokes all the way to the common room. Lauren smiled despite herself. It felt so long since she'd had anyone to joke with. By the time they went through the common room door, she was laughing out loud.

She pulled her kit bag off Ethan's shoulders and gave him a friendly punch.

"Thanks. You're just what I needed to cheer me up." She grinned.

Then a movement caught her eye. Katie, her eyes glistening, crossed the room and pushed out past Ethan and Lauren without a word.

Chapter Sixteen

Grace floated down the corridor, on her way to watch the end of Miss Radcliffe's class with the Year Nine girls. The boys were in a different class that morning with Mr Holt.

Grace wished she could do more to help Lauren. Over the last few days, she'd seen Katie snub her a few times by making excuses about having to be elsewhere every time Lauren tried to talk to her. Uncharacteristically, Katie had even taken to standing with Allison and *her* special friends in class. And Allison could be so mean when she wanted to be. She was queen of scathing looks and knowing smiles, and Grace's heart went out to Lauren.

In fact, Grace thought, Lauren looked thin and peaky, as if she wasn't taking care of herself or sleeping properly. Not even Nyree's attempts to cheer her up seemed to work. Though that was probably because Lauren still suspected Nyree of being the rumour-monger. Even though Grace had assured her that all Nyree did in the library was study equations so baffling that Grace had wondered if Nyree was truly human at all.

And what about Jay? Grace thought as she drifted past the posters of past shows and former students that adorned the walls. He had been keen on Lauren last term. But even he seemed to be keeping his distance. It was all very complicated.

Grace was so deep in thought that she almost melted right through a young woman who was walking towards her. Grace pulled up short. Who was this? She wasn't a student with all that turquoise hair peeping out from beneath a trilby hat. She was wearing a short tunic dress over black tights and heavy lace-up boots. Over the top, she had a leather jacket decorated with studs and chains.

Grace was even more intrigued when the woman knocked on Mrs Herriott's office door.

Abandoning all thoughts of watching the end of class, Grace melted through the wall so she could listen in. Mrs Herriott called, “Come in,” and the woman turned the handle and opened the door.

"Mrs Herriott?" The woman strode towards the desk with her hand outstretched, ready to shake. "My name is Piper Lapiz and I'm from UK News," she said in a strong, confident voice.

Mrs Herriott's eyebrows rose. She inclined her head and gestured to the chair on the opposite side of the desk. "Have a seat," she said. "How can I help you?"

Piper Lapiz sat and pulled a laptop out of the black leather satchel she had been carrying. "My newspaper has been following one of your students who seems to be finding some fascinating stuff about Amberwood Hall," she began as she opened the lid and typed in a code. Mrs Herriott's eyebrows rose further. "He's a member of an online group that deals with the paranormal, and he posts some excellent info. With your permission, I'd like to interview him, and maybe a few of the other students. We want to run a feature article!"

Piper turned her laptop to face the headmistress.

Grace swooped in behind Mrs Herriott to get a good look. She saw what looked like the front page of a newspaper. The headline read:

UK NEWS
"Haunted Amberwood!
Is Amberwood Hall Ballet School home to the famous Willis of Giselle?
Or does it have its own resident ghosts?"
by Piper Lapiz

There was no text underneath, but Piper explained. "If I could talk to the students, and maybe take some photos," she said, "particularly the ones who are involved in the ghost-hunting, we could angle the article on whether Amberwood Hall is haunted or not. People love ghost stories and I think we could make it unique by linking it to the fact that this is a ballet school. Lots of ballets use ghosts as a theme, don't they? It would be super cool, and great publicity for you."

Grace's form swelled and shimmered. She gritted her teeth to stop herself from crying out and giving this Piper woman hard evidence.

Mrs Herriott cleared her throat and shuffled some papers on her desk. Then she steepled her fingers and looked long and hard at Piper. "I know media people think that any publicity is good publicity," she said politely, "but I'm afraid

I'm not of the same opinion. I would rather my school wasn't turned into a subject of curiosity over the rumour that it might be haunted."

Piper shifted in her seat. Grace relaxed her jaw and breathed, "*Yes*!" She wished she could throw her arms around the headmistress and give her a grateful hug.

"We do serious work here," Mrs Herriott continued. "And I would be delighted for you to report on any aspect of that. But to make a feature of what is merely a teenage boy's fanciful pastime is, I think, stretching belief beyond reason."

Mrs Herriott stood up and walked towards the door. "Soon, our Houses are holding a Choreographics Competition. These are ballets that the students are choreographing and performing with no staff influence. If you would like to do a feature on that, you will be welcome. Bring your camera and notebook! But I cannot let you interview any student on the subject of ghosts."

The headmistress opened the door and looked expectantly at Piper, who stood up and fumbled as she stashed her laptop back in her satchel.

With face burning, she reached the door in three strides. Mrs Herriott held out her hand to shake. "The performance is on the 23rd," she said with a cool smile. "I will save you a seat!"

"Thank you," Piper murmured, shaking the head's hand. "I'll see if I'm available that evening."

Grace did a celebratory twirl and raced away to share the good news with Lauren. Maybe it would cheer her up.

When Grace reached the stable block, the boys' class was already over and they were rushing upstairs to change.

Grace melted into the studio, where the girls were still doing *brisés* from the corner, one at a time. The atmosphere in the studio was foggy with moisture-laden air caused by the perspiration pouring off the girls.

The last student to do the exercise was Lauren, and Grace sent her an encouraging smile as she launched into her jump. Lauren's face was grim, and she seemed to be struggling to get off the ground and make her back leg catch up to beat against the front one.

"Bring your weight forward, Lauren," Miss Radcliffe called. But Lauren looked like a sticky lump of wet clay. She didn't seem able to detach herself from the floor. She wiped the sweat out of her eyes and tried again. Her mouth was a thin line and her jaw rigid.

"Leave it now," Miss Radcliffe said as Lauren finally made it to the end of the diagonal line. "Come and do your *reverence*, girls. We're a bit late. Lauren, please stay behind."

Lauren nodded and looked at the floor. Grace floated beside her and whispered, *"Cheer up. I've got some good news for you!"*

The other girls trooped out after the class, laughing and chattering, but not before they sent a few sideways glances in Lauren's direction.

Lauren gathered up her things and pulled on a sweatshirt. When everyone had gone, she went and stood in front of the teacher.

Miss Radcliffe put her hand on Lauren's arm. "You look like you have the weight of the world on your shoulders, Lauren. You know, if you have a problem, it's always better to share it," she urged. "And if you want any help, you only have to tell me. Or anyone on the staff, for that matter."

Grace bobbed her head encouragingly at Lauren, but Lauren avoided looking at her.

"I'm fine, Miss Radcliffe," she insisted. "I just didn't sleep very well last night, so I'm tired."

Miss Radcliffe frowned, but didn't push. "All right. But I hate to see your work suffer, Lauren. Tell Matron I said you need a couple of early nights."

Lauren nodded and made her escape, with Grace hovering beside her.

The dressing room was still busy. Nyree, already dressed and halfway to the outer door, called to Lauren that she had left something in the library and was going to fetch it. Lauren barely acknowledged her. She changed in one corner, all by herself. No one else spoke to her and she didn't speak to anyone. Grace's heart ached for her friend. How could this person calling themselves the Secret Detective cause so much deliberate damage? Gossip was like poison, ruining everything it touched.

Grace kept quiet till they were walking back across the grounds and they were alone. Then she told Lauren about the journalist and how Mrs Herriott had sent her packing.

"That's not her, is it?" asked Lauren, pointing to a woman with turquoise hair, standing next to a 4x4 in the car park. She was talking to Alfie.

Grace gasped. *"Yes! Why is she talking to Alfie? Wait there!"* And she swooped across the lawn to listen.

"Yes, I'm positive the cellar is haunted," Grace heard Alfie saying as she got nearer. "Loads of us have heard noises and my EMF went berserk when we went down that one time."

"Could you go again?" Piper asked. "With a few friends, and get some footage? If you get video on your phone, I can lift still photos from it. That way, I can choose what's best."

Alfie looked dubious. "Mrs Herriott has banned us from the cellar."

"But if you went in secret," Piper suggested, "and emailed me the videos, I could do a really great piece. I won't mention your name or get you into trouble, I promise."

Alfie's eyes gleamed. "I suppose we could go at night! I can think of one or two who might be up for it," he said. "But I could get found out if I send stuff to you. They can trace anything nowadays!"

Piper rummaged in her bag. "Take this," she said, handing a memory stick to Alfie. "Mrs Herriott has invited me to cover the Choreographics Competition. So I've got a valid excuse to come back, and you can give it to me then."

Horrified, Grace whooshed back to Lauren and filled her in. *"You've got to stop him, Lauren,"* she implored. *"Old Tom is in the cellar and he's too stubborn to leave and hide. It would be awful if Alfie's device really worked and he found him."*

"But what on earth can I do?" Lauren gasped. "Alfie won't listen to me! Can't you get Rodney to come back? He can stop the device from working."

"He can, but remember what he did last time? He thinks it's funny to make it bleep and screech. It's probably better if he's not there! But you need to be. You must join in with anything Alfie plans so you can control what happens. Get

the device off him or something. Piper mustn't get any evidence!"

Chapter Seventeen

Lauren waited till Piper's car had drawn away, then she ran after Alfie to the common room. Nyree arrived at the same time, back from the library. They were just in time to hear Alfie gathering everyone together.

"Who wants to be part of another ghost hunt?" he called, his face glowing with excitement.

"Where?"

"When?"

"Oooh, creepy!"

"Me!"

"Me!" came the various comments, and people rushed to his side. Allison pushed her way through the throng and stood at his shoulder.

"Have you heard from the newspaper?" she asked.

Alfie nodded. "The journalist is going to do a huge feature. I just need to get some footage for her." He grinned round at the gathered group. "So, I'm going back down the cellar," he declared, "but it'll have to be at night, so no one knows."

There was a ripple of nervous laughter.

Allison, after a moment's thought, put her hand on his arm and coiled a lock of her hair round her finger. "I'll come!" she purred. Then a few brave ones joined in.

"Me too!"

"Wouldn't miss it for the world!"

Lauren threw her bag onto a sofa. "You do all realise," she warned, "that if you get caught, you risk getting expelled. I don't think Mrs Herriott ever lifted the ban on being out of bed at night."

"Yes, it would be a stupid thing to do," Katie agreed.

Lauren took in a sharp breath. Katie was on her side! She darted her a grateful glance, but Katie turned away.

Mark backed them both up. "You must be crazy," he sneered. "Never mind getting caught. What about all the reports of noises that people keep hearing?"

"Scared, are you?" Jay teased.

Mark's cheeks turned red. "No, but you won't get me going down there in the middle of the night. Last time we went, Alfie's machine went ballistic. So there must be a ghost. Imagine what it might do to you! I wouldn't risk it."

Jay grinned. "Well, according to Alfie, ghosts can't hurt you. I'm in!"

Alfie gave him a high five. He stared round at all the expectant faces and rubbed his nose. "Lauren has a point, though," he said. "It could be dangerous. We mustn't get caught. So it would be better if it was a small group. Quieter. Four at the most."

"Well, I called dibs first," Jay insisted.

"And you're not going without me!" Ethan chipped in.

Katie gasped. "You hate the thought of ghosts," she pointed out. "You always steer clear of any places that you think are spooky. How on earth can you want to do this?"

Ethan replied without meeting her gaze. "This is different. It's an adventure."

"We'll need at least one girl," Alfie pointed out. "To unlock the door from inside the house. She needn't come down to the cellar if she doesn't want to."

"How will you get the key?" Mark challenged.

"If you'd listened during the last fire drill," Alfie retorted, "you would know that Mrs Rowland always hangs the key on a hook at the hinge side of the door. So that whoever gets there first, if there's a fire, can find it."

Mark shrugged.

Lauren suddenly realised there was another flaw in Alfie's plan. Maybe it would be enough to stop him. "Hang on a minute," she said, "if this journalist is going to print pictures, how are we going to explain ourselves to Mrs Herriott?"

Allison took a step backwards and let go of Alfie's arm. A small frown appeared on her face.

Alfie pursed his lips. "I'll tell Piper she has to blur our faces," he announced after a moment's thought. Allison's nose wrinkled. She took another step backwards.

Lauren gritted her teeth. She would have to volunteer if she was to keep her promise to Grace. "All right, I'll do it," she said boldly.

"You were dead against it a minute ago," Allison exclaimed. "How come you've changed your tune now?"

Ethan spoke quickly. "I think that's a great idea," he said. "Lauren's less likely to lose her head and chicken out at the last moment."

Katie spun away and Lauren's heart sank further.

"Agreed," said Alfie. "So, me, Jay, Ethan and Lauren. We'll do it on the night before the choreographics."

That was clever, thought Lauren. It meant Alfie could off-load the memory stick the next day and reduce his risk of being caught.

Allison tossed her hair behind her shoulders. "I think you're mad," she scoffed, glaring at Lauren. "At least the boys have each other for company. I actually wouldn't want to be in your shoes." She shuddered for more effect. "You'll be creeping around all on your own in the dead of night."

"No, she won't," Nyree declared. "I shall keep her company."

Allison snorted. "Well then. What more could you want? Ghosts and aliens!" She twirled a finger next to her temple before turning away.

Lauren knew she should stick up for Nyree. After all, she had just rushed to her aid. But she couldn't let go of her suspicions that Nyree was in fact the Secret Detective. So she merely shot her a sympathetic smile.

The following week, Lauren fretted over the thought that she had volunteered for a ghost hunt and risked getting expelled, instead of spending more time finding out who had posted the nasty rumours. The only good thing, she thought grimly, was that there hadn't been any for a while.

But that didn't seem to be helping her situation with Katie. They hadn't spoken to each other for days. Katie always seemed to be asleep when Lauren got into bed at night, and she stood at opposite ends of the barre in class and never looked at Lauren. In lessons, when they had always sat together, Katie now made sure there was never a spare seat next to her. She suddenly seemed to have a whole new gang of friends.

Like now, Lauren thought moodily as they waited for Mr Holt to start the class. Katie was chatting to Allison and Emily while they stretched their legs along the top barre. Nicola was hanging onto every word and warming her feet by walking on the spot. Nyree was practising standing like a statue. Not even the boys were trying to include Lauren, despite rallying to support her in the ghost hunting matter.

She was alone. She picked at the hairnet round her bun and tried to look as if she didn't have a care in the world. But her stomach was churning, and her eyes felt like they could fill up at any minute.

Mr Holt breezed in, clapping his hands for attention. "We're going to do something different today," he announced. Was it Lauren's imagination or did he look at her when he said it? "But first, barre! *Pliés*!"

Everyone scrambled into position and the music started. Lauren threw herself into the exercise and tried to forget her sadness. She might be losing her best friend, but no one could take her dancing away from her.

Half an hour later, and the barre work finished, Mr Holt called them into the centre.

"Today, we're going to do some free interpretation!" he said. The students looked at each other and raised eyebrows. "Totally free! You're going to interpret the music as you hear it. No stopping to work out steps. Just dance."

He walked between them. "Choose partners," he called as he steered the people nearest him towards each other. Allison made a bee-line for Alfie. Nyree, never more than a metre away, took Lauren's hand.

"No, no," Mr Holt chided, approaching at a jog. "You go with Suzie, Nyree. I want Lauren to partner Katie."

Lauren's head shot up, and she met Katie's eyes across the studio. Neither of them moved.

Mr Holt went to the music system and plugged in his phone. The pianist raised a questioning eyebrow and flicked through music books. "You can have a rest," Mr Holt told her. "I'm going to play Mussorgsky's Night on a Bare Mountain."

"Mm, very dramatic!" She smiled.

Mr Holt beamed at the class. "Here's what I want you to do. At first, I want you to mirror each other. One person will lead, the other will copy. Let's do it alphabetically, on first names. That person will begin. Then, when I clap, you swap. And when I clap again, you dance together. Let it flow. Use the moves you used originally, or any other moves, but keep it TOGETHER. Let's see what you come up with!"

Lauren and Katie stared at each other from opposite sides of the room. Neither of them moved to be nearer, unlike the others, who had all claimed a small area of the floor to work on.

The first bars of the music swelled. Katie peeled herself away from the wall and, keeping her head averted, began to walk around the perimeter, in time to the music. Her arms rose slowly and gracefully at her sides till the outside of her wrists were touching above her head. Lauren copied, never taking her eyes off Katie. Katie lunged and swept her arms in a wide circle. Lauren imitated her on the opposite side of the studio.

The music intensified, and Katie turned towards Lauren. Her eyes flashed with anger. She thrust her hands out as if pleading, then she swirled away in a series of free turns with her back arching and her hands imploring towards the ceiling. Lauren followed, oblivious to the couples who were dodging to get out of the way. She focused totally on Katie, who didn't look at her at all.

Katie's movements increased in speed and fury along with the tempo. Her forehead wore a constant frown and her jaw was rigid. Lauren kept up. As the storm on the mountain grew in the frenzied music, Lauren felt the storm in her own heart brimming to the surface. She thrust her arms into the positions that Katie chose, as though trying to direct her energy across the room to her distant friend.

They weaved in and out of the other dancers, who faltered. One or two stopped their own work to watch. Mr Holt didn't reprimand them.

He clapped the signal to change. Lauren and Katie froze, then Katie's eyes found Lauren's, and they glared at each other. Lauren began to lead.

She moved across the centre of the room towards Katie. Katie had no choice but to copy. Lauren thrust her arm to the side and followed it with her body, ending in a circular sweep that took her body to the floor. She arched her back and bent her knees before using her core to bring herself to her feet again on a dramatic chord in the music. She felt the tension release through her body, along with a rush of air from her lungs. She glanced at Katie, whose face was still tight and angry.

Lauren spun away, barely noticing that she had the entire room to move in. Everyone had stopped dancing except for her and Katie.

The drama in the music built and Lauren moved faster, spinning on the build-ups, leaping on the crashing chords. Suddenly Mr Holt clapped again.

They had to dance together.

Lauren turned on one foot and held a pose on her toes, with her other foot under her knee, her arms outstretched like she was casting a spell.

Katie did the same. Then the two girls ran towards each other in fury. Their hands met, and they spun each other round till they were both dizzy. Katie thrust Lauren away and leaped towards the corner. Lauren pirouetted and used drag runs to catch her up and pull her back to the centre.

Twisting and turning in time to the music, they fought. They chased each other from one side of the studio to the other, sliding across the floor until Katie, with a strength Lauren never knew she possessed, threw Lauren to the floor and, grasping both her hands, spun her round in a circle while Lauren arched and twisted, contracted and stretched her body in time to the increasing crescendo of the orchestra. Cymbals clashed and Lauren leaped to her feet. The music rose to its climax as she grabbed Katie's waist.

Katie arched backwards, glaring, and Lauren saw that her eyes were glistening with unshed tears.

Lauren let her go. Katie staggered and Lauren's hand shot out to steady her. At the very peak of the music's crescendo, the two girls fell together in a tight hug.

Morning broke on the mountain. The music steadied and calmed. Breathing heavily, Lauren and Katie swayed with its gentler rhythm. They didn't let go of each other as they continued to move around the room, their heads on each other's shoulders. Lauren sobbed into Katie's neck and she felt Katie's tears soaking her own. As the bells in the music died away, they sank to one knee, the other leg stretched out behind, perfectly mirrored. Their arms remained tightly entwined and their heads buried.

No one spoke.

Chapter Eighteen

Lauren didn't know how long she and Katie sobbed into each other's shoulders. She only knew she didn't want to let go, and it seemed that Katie felt the same.

Eventually, Lauren raised her head and saw a blurry Mr Holt crouching beside her and Katie. Dazed, she looked around the room and realised it was empty of students. When had Mr Holt dismissed them?

She wiped her eyes so the teacher came into focus. He was smiling. He held out his hands and helped the girls to their feet.

"I have some very special homework for you both," he said gently. "I want you to find a quiet place and take turns to talk. Don't speak over each other but listen to each other. Find out what's gone wrong between you."

Lauren drew in a shuddery breath and heard Katie do the same.

Mr Holt squeezed their shoulders. "You might still disagree at the end of the conversation," he continued, "but you need to give each other a chance to talk and listen properly. Off you go now. And well done."

Lauren and Katie gathered their belongings. They didn't want to join the throng in the dressing room, so they took their time. When they finally went to get changed, most people had rushed away for lunch.

"Why don't we go to the attic studio?" Lauren suggested in a low voice. "No one will disturb us there. Everyone thinks it's haunted now."

Katie nodded and gave her a shaky smile. "It's where you showed me how to do better beats when we first came to Amberwood," she whispered.

"I know," Lauren smiled.

The girls pulled on their outdoor gear and started towards the door. A movement caught Lauren's eye and Nyree, the only person left in the dressing room, appeared at Lauren's side.

"You can't come with me right now," Lauren told her. "Go and get some lunch. Katie and I want to talk on our own."

Nyree stared at her, then turned her head and walked away in the opposite direction. Lauren felt bad for being so short with her, but she would say sorry later. Right now, she had to focus on Katie.

The two girls sprinted across the grounds to the house and up the stairs to the attic studio. When Lauren pushed open the door, she saw Grace floating in the centre.

The ghost smiled in welcome, then opened her eyes wide in surprise when Katie followed Lauren into the room. Lauren gave a tiny warning shake of her head and Grace withdrew into the shadows.

"Phew, it's dustier than ever in here!" Katie commented.

"It'll brush off," Lauren said, sitting on the floor in a corner and leaning back against the wall. "I'm shattered!" she admitted.

Katie sat down beside her. "Me too. Are we a couple of numpties or what?" She took a deep breath and ran her hand through her hair. "Let's do what Mr Holt said. You go first."

Lauren wasn't sure she wanted to go first. She didn't really know what to say. Haltingly, she began. "I... I don't really understand why you thought I would try to steal Ethan off you." She faltered.

"You..." Katie began, but Lauren held up her hand.

"One at a time, remember?" Katie nodded and Lauren continued. "Every single thing in those messages is a lie." She felt herself getting more confident. "And I don't know why you believed them. I know you think there's no smoke without fire, but you wouldn't even let me explain."

She stopped. Katie was sitting forward, clearly eager to put her own case. Lauren gestured for her to go ahead.

"You just seemed to be with Ethan all the time. The way you danced with him at the party, the way you were looking at him when he was carrying your bag from rehearsals."

Lauren opened her mouth to protest, and it was Katie's turn to hold up her hand. "I know," she said. "It was nothing. And I wasn't angry because I thought you were trying to steal Ethan. People can't steal each other! You already worked that out last year when you were so upset over your dad."

Lauren remembered but kept quiet.

"What really upset me," Katie continued, "was that I thought you weren't being a good friend to me. I felt let down. And that was because I listened to other people instead of letting you tell your own truth. Things started getting bigger and bigger in my mind and I couldn't back down."

"I should have tried harder too," Lauren admitted. "I allowed myself to feel angry because you wouldn't believe me, instead of seeing it from your point of view."

Katie smiled a wry smile. "Remember what Ethan told us his dad always says? " She looked at Lauren from under her brow.

Lauren grinned and together they chanted, "Be Bigger Than Them!"

Lauren felt the last tendrils of tension drift away. Grace floated in closer and gave her a thumbs up.

"What we still don't know is, who is inventing these rumours?" Katie twisted a lock of hair. "I know Allison's always had it in for you, but this is affecting three of us, and I don't think it's really her style. Amberwood never used to be filled with such malicious whispers!"

And Nyree didn't use to be at Amberwood, Lauren thought. But she kept it to herself. Until she had proof, she wouldn't say anything. Otherwise she was just making assumptions. Which was exactly what had got her and Katie into this mess.

"We did say," she said instead, "that we would ask Mark if he can trace which computer the messages are coming from. But we never did. Shall we do it now?"

"Good idea," said Katie, heaving herself to her feet and brushing the dust off her jogging pants.

The two girls looked at each other for a second, then hugged.

"Let's not fall out again, please?" Lauren whispered, and Katie agreed.

Feeling lighter and happier than they had for weeks, they ran to the common room and found Mark sitting with Alfie and Ethan. Nyree was doing homework nearby and Lauren didn't want her to hear what they were saying, so she asked Mark if she and Katie could speak to him in private. The three of them went out into the corridor.

Mark's face, which had lit up at being singled out, soon clouded over when Lauren explained their idea. He blew out his cheeks. "I don't know how to do that," he admitted. "It's way beyond my capabilities. I doubt anyone in this school would know, to be honest." And he turned abruptly and went back to the other boys.

Lauren sighed. "So much for that idea!"

"What idea?" said a new voice.

Lauren looked round to see Jay striding towards them. She opened her mouth to speak, but he held up his hand to stop her. "Doesn't matter," he said. "I have something far more important to tell you. Julian wants you to go for a special rehearsal after tea tonight. Studio Four."

Lauren's eyes opened wide. "What for? I've got that puppet dance down to the last step. It's not as if it's difficult. He can't think I need more practice."

Jay put his finger against his nose and tapped. "You'll find out," he said mysteriously. "Just be prepared for some changes!" And he slipped into the common room before Lauren could ask any more.

Chapter Nineteen

As she got ready for bed on the night before the competition, Lauren tried to calm her thumping heart. She still couldn't quite believe what Jay had managed to do on her behalf. Thanks to his suggestion that Lauren could do more with her role than the current choreography allowed, Julian had let her develop something that felt fresh and modern and exciting. There hadn't been time to learn a whole new choreography, but he'd let Lauren come up with lots of changes of her own, including a much more demanding section. Julian had been so supportive and interested in new ideas that Lauren had started to feel guilty for being so dismissive about him.

"I don't know whether I'm excited about the competition, or terrified that I might be expelled before I get to dance," she confessed to Katie as they brushed their teeth side by side at the sinks.

Katie shivered. "I wish you weren't going tonight, Lauren," she said. "You could have let one of the others do it. Or at least unlock the door, then come back to bed. Leave them to it!"

Lauren couldn't explain why she had to be there without telling Katie about the ghosts, and she knew she couldn't do that. So she shrugged. "I suppose it's better that there's someone sensible there to keep the boys in check," she said. She glanced sideways at her constant shadow and tilted her head. "And I won't be totally alone. You can keep a look-out for staff, can't you, Nyree?"

"Of course," replied Nyree solemnly. "I can hide better than you too, because my face won't shine in the dark like yours."

Lauren and Katie burst out laughing.

"What's so funny?" Nyree asked, her eyes like saucers. "It's physics. The light doesn't reflect off my skin like it does off yours. It's all to do with the..."

"Stop!" Lauren giggled, holding up her hand. "It doesn't matter. I just need to know you've got my back."

Lauren didn't need an alarm to wake up at the allotted time; she had asked Grace to come and wake her. And the ghost did so, promptly. Lauren slipped on her dressing gown and gently shook Nyree.

Nyree's eyes opened, and she sat bolt upright. She nodded at Lauren and reached for her own dressing gown. Then the two girls slipped out of the dorm and into the corridor.

Lauren led the way, glad of the faint light from the sensors on the emergency lighting that meant they didn't need a torch. They crept down the stairs. Grace floated alongside them. To Lauren's surprise Rodney was waiting at the bottom of the stairs. He tipped his cap at Lauren, but for once didn't make any wisecracks.

Lauren hoped that Grace had managed to convince the stable boy how important it was that the detector didn't detect this time. They had to protect Old Tom at all costs.

The two ghosts took the lead, checking there were no staff patrolling the corridors, with Rodney tiptoeing exaggeratedly. Lauren had to stifle a nervous giggle as she and Nyree slipped from doorway to doorway.

When they got to the back door, Lauren reached out and slipped the key off its hook. She had checked out Alfie's information days ago, so she knew exactly where to look. She slipped it into the lock and turned it. At the click, she grabbed the handle and opened the door without a sound.

Alfie, Ethan and Jay were waiting on the other side, muffled up in scarves and gloves against the chilly night.

In single file, they padded along the corridors. The eerie silence weighed heavily as they darted between dark doorways and alcoves. When they got near the kitchen, Lauren put her finger to her lips. It would be just their luck that some member of staff would be there, sneaking in a midnight snack.

But all was clear. They continued to the cellar door. Lauren breathed out her relief when that opened silently as well, and they slipped inside. She stretched out her hand to turn on the light, but Alfie stopped her.

"There'll be enough light from the video camera," he whispered. "And it'll be more atmospheric without an electric light."

He crept in front and inched down the stairs backwards, filming the others as they descended.

They were only halfway down when they heard a soft knocking noise. Despite being best friends with Amberwood's ghosts, Lauren's heart missed a beat. Ethan gasped and Jay froze mid-step. Alfie swung the camera around and the spotlight illuminated the main room in the cellar.

"I'm not so sure about this after all," Ethan whispered.

But Alfie beckoned to them to continue.

Lauren heard the rustle of a newspaper, and she glanced towards the remnants of the boiler. Old Tom scowled at her from over the front page. Lauren could just make out the headlines in the light from the camera:

Friday 10 June 1870

DEATH OF MR CHARLES DICKENS

"More interruptions," grumbled Old Tom. *"Why can't you children leave me in peace?"*

Lauren wanted to apologise, but of course, she couldn't say a word. Grace swooped across and explained in a voice that clearly showed she was the Young Lady of the House.

"*We won't be long, Tom. They're just trying to prove our existence. But Rodney won't let the machine work. And once they think there are no ghosts here, they'll leave*."

Old Tom snorted and shook his newspaper again.

Alfie spoke into the camera. He sounded so serious that Lauren would have laughed if she hadn't been so nervous.

"Here we are in the cellar of Amberwood Hall," Alfie said in his best reporter's voice. "I will now engage my EMF detector."

While he held onto the camera with one hand and fumbled in his coat pocket with the other, Lauren looked round the room. Something was different. Was it those suitcases? Had they been piled like that before?

Alfie finally freed the detector from the depths of his pocket and showed it to the camera. Then, one-handed, he tried to switch it on.

Nyree pushed past Lauren and snatched the detector from Alfie's hand. "You can't film and do the detector," she stated. "I'll do it."

Too late, Lauren realised *she* could have done that. Then she could have made sure it was switched off. But not to worry, she was sure Rodney would play his part.

She directed a pleading glance towards the stable boy. He nodded and hovered near to Nyree.

So far, so good. There was no sound at all as she swept the room with the machine. Even when it passed over Old Tom and Grace, who was clutching her throat, it was silent.

Lauren glanced gratefully at Rodney, but he shrugged. *"I'm not doing anything. I don't think they really work,"* he declared. He peered at the dark row of tiny lightbulbs.

Alfie was continuing to film the room, panning from one side to the other and keeping up a soft monologue. "If we wait a few minutes, I feel sure the EMF will detect a presence," he intoned. Beside the boiler, Old Tom rolled his eyes and shook his newspaper, more loudly this time.

The longer they waited, the more Lauren was afraid Rodney might get bored and change his mind about being sensible. And Old Tom wasn't trying to hide at all! She decided it was time she did something to distract them.

"Guys," she called softly, "I don't remember those suitcases being like that. Do you think someone's moved them?" She walked over to get a better look.

The cases were definitely not in the same places. In fact, as far as Lauren could see, it looked like someone had piled them like a wall to create a room.

"Alfie," she called, "bring the light over. This is really weird. It's like a cave here, but I can't see inside."

Suddenly a slow, ominous banging sounded from behind some abandoned scenery on the other side of the room. Everyone jumped and spun round. The sound of a chain clanking joined the banging. Lauren's eyes darted to Rodney, but he was hovering next to Grace, looking as puzzled as she was.

Alfie zoomed in on the scenery. "Point the detector this way," he called in a loud whisper.

But Ethan grabbed his arm. "Let's get out of here," he said, his voice shaky. "I really don't like this."

Jay backed him up. "Ethan's right. I think we've been here long enough." He took a step towards the stairs.

Even though that was exactly what Lauren wanted them to do, she was curious about the cases. Ten more seconds wouldn't matter. "It's probably just the central heating pipes," she insisted. "Let's just look at this before we go." And she grabbed the camera off Alfie and shone it into the cubicle formed by the suitcases.

"What the...?" The light from the camera fell on a laptop balancing on four cases piled on top of each other to make a table. A cable snaked up the wall and through an air grid to the outside.

The laptop was open, but the screen was black. Lauren pressed the power button, and it sprang directly into life. Directly onto the Gossip Wall of the school magazine.

The avatar of the Secret Detective stared at them from the screen.

Chapter Twenty

Everyone crowded into the opening and stared in silence at the laptop. Then Lauren noticed a distinctive red and yellow patterned bag propped against the side of the cases.

She rounded on Nyree. "It is you! I knew it! That's your laptop case, isn't it? And that must be your laptop."

Nyree's mouth fell open and she stared at Lauren. Her usually inexpressive eyes reflected her hurt and anger. "It's not mine!" she protested. "How could you think that? What do you mean, you knew it?"

"I've suspected it for ages," Lauren argued. "And here's the proof. You can't deny that's your laptop case."

"But anyone could get a bag like that," Nyree cried. "It's not handmade! Alfie here admired it. So did Mark. Lots of people like it."

They were interrupted by the sound of a soft scuffle from behind the scenery, over on the dark side of the room.

"What's that?" Ethan gasped.

Lauren squeezed past him to shine the camera light, but before she could, one of the scenery flats fell to the floor with a resounding crash. Footsteps pounded on the stone, making for the stairs.

Lauren swung the light round just as Grace raised her hand and caused the cellar door to slam shut. Jay sprinted to the electric light switch and snapped it on.

They all looked towards the top of the stairs. Cowering in the sudden flood of light, and unable to escape, was Mark.

The boys ran up and grabbed him. They dragged him back into the room, and Jay held onto his arms while the others confronted him.

"Let me go," Mark seethed, writhing to get out of Jay's grasp. But Jay was one of the strongest boys in Year Nine and Mark was helpless against him.

"What are you doing here?" Alfie demanded. "How did you even get in here in the middle of the night?"

Mark squirmed. "I've got a back door key," he admitted. "I borrowed Mrs Rowland's key one weekend and got a copy cut in town."

"Why?" Lauren challenged.

"I was trying to give you something for the video," Mark muttered. "I thought it would be fun."

Alfie's shoulders sagged. "So there's nothing here after all," he said, defeated. "Just you, making spooky noises."

Grace and Rodney punched the air and grinned with relief. Old Tom rolled his eyes and shook his head.

"Exactly," said Mark. He looked at them each in turn. "Don't you think we'd better scarper before someone hears us?" His eyes flickered to the pile of suitcases where Nyree was still standing like a statue.

Lauren stared at Mark and narrowed her eyes. He was lying.

She felt the colour drain from her face as the jigsaw suddenly fell into place in her head. Mark had the IT knowledge to do what the Secret Detective had been doing. He was at the Valentine's party, and he could have been on the stairs when she was talking to Ethan about Katie that day. And although he wasn't dancing in the choreographic competition, there was nothing stopping him from seeing them in breaks during rehearsals, because the boys' dormitories were in the stable block.

"You weren't trying to give Alfie material for the video, were you?" she said softly. "You were trying to scare us away. Because of what you were doing here."

She put the video camera on the makeshift table and gestured to the laptop. "It's yours, isn't it?"

Mark tried to twist away then he wilted and nodded miserably.

Lauren continued in a strangled voice. "You're the Secret Detective, the one who's posted all that stupid fake news about me and Ethan."

"What?" Alfie, Ethan and Jay all gasped together. Jay let go of Mark's wrists and they stared at their classmate in horror.

"Why on earth would you do that?" Ethan demanded. "Do you know how many people you hurt? How could you be so stupid?"

Mark's face had gone crimson. He looked at his feet and said nothing.

Lauren stared at him. "Unbelievable!" she breathed. She clenched her fists, fighting a desire to pummel him.

Mark shifted uneasily.

"I think we should go," Jay said. "We've made enough noise." He sent Lauren a sympathetic look. "We'll deal with Mark back at the dorm," he assured her, and he picked up the laptop and bag to take with them.

Lauren swallowed and glanced at Nyree. She was standing motionless, her eyes wide and glistening. Lauren had never seen her look so sad.

"I... I'll stay here with Nyree and put the cases back where they should be," Lauren said, clutching at the first thing she could think of. She needed time to process what had happened and make things right with Nyree before they went back to bed. And they wouldn't be able to talk in the dorm.

"Are you crazy?" Ethan hissed. "What about the ghosts?"

Lauren gave a dismissive wave of her hand. "There aren't any ghosts, are there?" she said with a tight laugh. "It was Mark all along."

The boys muttered among themselves, but finally let Lauren have her way. They marched Mark up the stairs, telling Lauren she needn't worry about locking the door, they would use Mark's key.

As soon as they'd gone, Lauren turned to Nyree and took her hands. "Nyree, I'm sorry." She swallowed hard. "I was just so desperate to find someone guilty and you're so clever with computers and everything..." She ran out of steam.

Nyree raised huge tear-filled eyes to Lauren. "How could you think anything so horrible of me?" she sniffed. "I thought you were my friend. I would never do anything to hurt you."

Lauren cringed. "I know, and I was so wrong. I'd got it into my head that you were doing it when you were alone in the library. I was carried away with a stubborn idea and no proof." A bit like Katie with me, she thought, and felt even worse.

Nyree continued to sniff. Lauren glanced at Grace for support. Grace looked stricken, and even Rodney's cheerful face had clouded over. They floated nearer.

"How can I make it up to you?" Lauren asked eventually, though she couldn't imagine anything she could say that would help. She remembered all the times Nyree had stuck up for her and been around when she needed company. In fact, Lauren thought, she wasn't so bad, really. Just different.

Nyree drew in her breath and blew it out again with a huge sigh. "It's okay," she said. "I forgive you. It must have been awful, being the subject of all those rumours. I wonder why Mark did it?"

Lauren snorted. "I intend to find that out tomorrow," she declared. "Come on, let's go."

Nyree held back. "There is just one thing that's puzzling me. Can I ask you?"

Lauren nodded.

Nyree leaned closer. "Why didn't Old Tom tell Grace and Rodney what Mark was doing?" she asked in a stage whisper. "We could have had the answer ages ago, and you and Katie would never have fallen out."

Lauren reeled. Rodney and Grace darted behind Lauren so they were facing Nyree.

"You can see us?" Grace exclaimed.

Nyree nodded. "Of course. I always see ghosts. I've been seeing them all my life. My gran did too."

"Why didn't you say something?" Lauren asked, incredulous.

"Gran told me it was rude to interrupt other people's conversations," she said. "And that I must never speak to a ghost till they speak to me first. Grace and Rodney never spoke to me." She looked directly at the two ghosts, a rare smile brightening her face.

Lauren grinned. Why was she not surprised? Nyree always took orders literally. "Well, you're amazing for not telling anyone," she said. "Especially with all the talk of ghosts and Alfie's ghost hunting. You could have proved him right hundreds of times."

"As soon as I saw you never told anyone, I knew I had to keep the secret too," Nyree pointed out. "Anyway, I hate the way Alfie is trying to find the ghosts and threaten their existence. They're your friends. And this is their home. They were here first."

Lauren didn't know what to say. This girl was full of surprises.

"In fact," Nyree continued, "that's why I wanted to hold the ghost-o-meter. I'm not sure they really work, but they certainly can't when they're switched off!"

Grace touched her hand to her heart. "Thank you, Nyree," she said. "You are now officially allowed to talk to us whenever you like. Unless other people are around!"

Nyree's face glowed with delight, and Lauren grinned too. It would be nice having someone else who knew about the ghosts.

Old Tom rattled his newspaper and grunted. "Can't you youngsters find somewhere else to have your party?" he growled.

Lauren looked at him. "Sorry," she said. "Why didn't you tell Grace and Rodney about the hidden laptop? Mark must have been down here loads of times!"

Old Tom scowled. "I didn't know what the boy was up to, did I?" he said. "None of my business what you lot do. Now clear off all of you. This is my cellar."

Grace floated towards the stairs and beckoned to the others to follow. "Tom wouldn't know what a laptop was, anyway," she whispered. "Or a Gossip Wall! So we must excuse him."

The ghosts melted through the door before Lauren could open it. Then Grace drifted back to tell her the coast was clear.

Keeping close to the walls, the two girls hurried back to the dorm and into their beds.

Nyree leaned over to whisper to Lauren before they went to sleep. "What do you think we should do about Mark?"

Lauren whispered back. "I don't know, but I intend to make sure he apologises and puts things right."

Chapter Twenty-One

In the dormitory the next morning, everyone clamoured around, wanting to know how the ghost-hunting adventure had gone.

Lauren brushed off their questions. "It was exactly as I thought it would be," she said. "A non-event and a total waste of time. Not to mention a waste of precious sleep." She wasn't going to tell anyone about Mark, not even Katie. First, she wanted to find out why he'd done it. Then she wanted him to confess himself.

"Well, at least you didn't get caught," Katie pointed out.

Allison snorted. "I can’t believe she got away with it!"

"Seriously, Allison?" Lauren asked. "You still want me to get expelled?"

Allison had the grace to blush. "Of course not," she snapped. And she flounced out with her wash bag.

People asked a few more questions, but Lauren fended them off, and Nyree backed her up. Eventually, they lost interest. Far better things were happening at Amberwood that day, and the entire school was buzzing with excitement. Even though not everyone was dancing in the competition, most people were involved with scenery, lighting, costumes or make-up.

Lauren was looking forward to it now that she was no longer an old-fashioned clown. Thanks to Jay's intervention with Julian, she was a superhero puppet with moves and sequences inspired by her and Katie's dance-fight. Her costume was a flattering black cat-suit that made her look like Black Widow from the Avengers, and Julian had even agreed that she should dance en pointe. She had had great fun in the art room, dyeing her pointe shoes black.

Breakfast that morning was a help-yourself affair. Lauren yawned as she filled a bowl with cereal. She wished she hadn't been awake half the night. It was going to be a very full evening, with each choreography like a mini ballet, lasting twenty minutes. There would be a ten-minute break in-between each one for scenery changes and a half-hour interval, like any full-length performance. Although no parents would be present, local students would pack the auditorium, as well as the Amberwood pupils who weren't on stage. And the judges were coming from other schools, which had everyone on edge with nerves. They wanted to show that Amberwood was the best school in the country!

The Year Nine boys clattered in a few minutes later and, following them at a distance and looking distinctly nervous, was Mark. He went and sat on his own on the other side of the dining room.

Lauren waited to see if the boys would say anything about the Secret Detective, but everyone was busy discussing the show. In the end, she asked Jay how they had left it.

"Don't worry," Jay muttered under his breath, "we really laid it on thick and now we've all agreed that's the end of it."

"Did you find out why he did it?" Lauren insisted.

Jay looked sheepish. "It didn't seem relevant really," he hedged. "What's done is done. He won't do it again."

Lauren wasn't satisfied. She looked over at Mark who was glancing anxiously in her direction, as though he was afraid she was going to tell everyone.

Trying to ignore Alfie, who was telling anyone who would listen that he didn't think they'd given the EMF device a fair trial, Lauren ate her breakfast at breakneck speed. Then she stood up.

Katie looked up. "That was quick!"

"Yeah, I've got something to do," Lauren said vaguely. "I'll catch you later." And she turned to the other side of the dining room, intent on catching Mark.

But he'd gone. Lauren blew out her cheeks and went looking for him. She tried all the most likely places, starting and ending with the common room,

Grace melted through the wood just as Lauren’s hand grasped the door handle.

"Oh, hello!" Lauren said. "Is Mark in there? I’ve been looking everywhere for him."

"He isn't," Grace replied. "But I did see him heading to the library."

"Thanks!" said Lauren. "Come with me?"

Grace nodded and Lauren set off at a lope towards the stairs with her friend floating by her side.

There was only one person in the library, and he was sitting with his head on a table cushioned by his folded arms.

Lauren squared her shoulders, strode over and tapped him on the shoulder.

Mark jumped. His chair scraped on the wooden floor and almost clattered over as he leapt up. His face burned bright red when he saw Lauren glaring at him. "Are... are you going to rat me out to everyone?" he stammered.

"That depends," Lauren growled. "First of all, tell me, what possessed you to do it? It must have taken so much planning – getting the key, setting yourself up in the cellar. Going there at night! What on earth was important enough to make you want to do all that?"

There was silence then Mark whispered, "Katie."

"What?" Lauren cried. "What's that supposed to mean. Katie was the one you were hurting most."

Mark slumped back into his chair. "I didn't mean to," he said. "I really like Katie. I thought if I could turn her against Ethan, she might like me instead."

Lauren couldn't speak. She stared at Mark with her mouth half open.

"Please don't tell her," Mark added.

Lauren laughed coldly. "Oh, I'm not going to," she said. And just as hope flickered in Mark's eyes she added, "You are."

Mark shifted in his seat. "You can't make me," he muttered.

"Oh, can't I?" Lauren was ruthless now. "Either you confess to Katie and apologise, or the entire school learns about your nasty little hobby. Either way, Katie will find out."

Mark groaned and buried his face in his hands. Lauren watched him for a moment.

Grace, who had remained silent until now, floated into her line of vision. *"I think you've convinced him,"* she said. *"Go and get Katie. I'll keep an eye on Mark."*

Lauren nodded. "Stay here," she snapped to Mark. "If you don't, I'll know." And she ran out of the library and back to the common room.

Poking her head round the door, she found Katie with her head in a book. Lauren went over to her. "Come with me," she said, snatching the book out of Katie's hand and marking the page before stuffing it into Katie's bag. "Mark has something to tell you!"

"Really?" Katie looked puzzled. "Can you give me a hint."

Lauren shook her head. "Nope."

Nyree appeared by her side as if by magic. Lauren looked down at her and grinned. "Yes, all right. You too!"

"Where are we going?" Katie panted as Lauren led them back to the library at a run.

Lauren pointed.

"What makes you think he's here on a Saturday?" Katie mused as they pushed open the door.

"Trust me," Lauren replied grimly.

They approached Mark who had returned to his slump with his head on his arms. Grace floated away to the window with an encouraging smile at Lauren.

"We're here," Lauren announced.

Mark stood up and backed away. He blushed again.

Intrigued, Katie smiled at him. "Lauren says you've got something to tell me," she said, tilting her head.

Mark shifted from one foot to the other. He gazed at the floor and muttered, "Sorry."

"Sorry? What for?" Katie frowned.

Mark's head shot up and Lauren's eyes bored into him. "I told you I wouldn't tell her," she said. "I won't tell anyone, not now you've stopped, but Katie deserves to hear the truth from you."

Mark's jaw tightened. He rubbed his forehead and took a deep breath. Then he confessed. "It was me. I'm the Secret Detective. I posted those rumours about Ethan and Lauren. I made it all up."

The colour drained out of Katie's face. "Why would you do such a dumb thing?"

"Because... I... I wanted you to stop liking Ethan and go out with me," he stammered. "I... I really like you. That's the only reason I did it."

Katie's jaw dropped and the blood slowly crept back into her cheeks, turning them pink. "I don't know what to say," she breathed. She turned to Lauren. "How did you find out?"

Lauren filled her in on what had happened the night before. Katie's eyes widened with each revelation, and she shook her head in disbelief. "So it wasn't a non-event, after all," she said.

Mark hung his head and for a few seconds, no one seemed to want to speak.

Nyree broke the silence. "And that's another thing," she queried. "Did you get a case like mine on purpose, to put suspicion on me?"

Mark looked horrified. "No, I swear! I told you from day one that I liked it. I just happened to see it in a charity shop when I was in town and bought it on the spur of the moment. I never meant to get you in trouble, not really."

Nyree looked sceptical but she let it go.

Lauren took charge. "Right. You've made your confession," she said. She pointed to his laptop, still in its case. "Now, fire it up," she commanded.

Mark pulled the machine out and opened it. He pressed the power button, and they waited for it to boot.

"You're going to post one more time as the Secret Detective," Lauren explained. "You're going to admit that everything you said was lies and that you won't be posting again."

Mark stared at Lauren. "I suppose you want me to confess my real name."

"Don't tempt me," Lauren said with a grimace. "But no. I think you're sorry, really. And you've already got five of us to face. You'll just have to hope that none of us tells."

Mark typed. He apologised for what he'd done and said it had been a silly joke, and he hadn’t meant to hurt anyone. Then he announced he wouldn't be posting, ever again, and wished everyone luck in the competition that evening. He turned the screen round so the girls could all read it.

"Good!" said Lauren. "Press go."

Mark complied and sat back, blowing out his cheeks.

"You know," Katie said gently, "it never works. You can't win someone by being nasty about other people."

Mark nodded miserably.

"Right, that's the end of it," Lauren declared. "It's time we all got to class."

Chapter Twenty-Two

Lauren stood in the wings, waiting for the stagehands to strike the scenery from the previous choreography. Her house, third in the programme, was next, directly after the interval. She couldn't wait to get on stage.

Eventually the set was ready. Lauren walked carefully to her place, holding up the wooden crossbar that was attached to the strings leading to her feet, wrists, and head. It was proving tricky not to get tangled up.

She lowered herself in front of a box that was like a small platform and arranged herself in a crumpled pose. A helper laid the crossbar on top of the box for her. Julian, as the toy shop owner, would stand on it and 'work' the puppet strings.

Lauren kept perfectly still. It was essential that she didn't dislodge the crossbar or detach the strings yet.

The auditorium lights went out and the buzz of chatter from the audience instantly ceased. The music began. There was a gentle swish as the curtain went up. The stage lights prevented the performers from seeing the audience, but Lauren knew Katie would be sitting on the edge of her seat, maybe gripping Ethan's and Jay's hands in excitement for her friend's performance. They had saved an entire row for Lizzie and the other Year Nines from the local school and Grace was hovering in the wings, always near when Lauren danced. Rodney looked down from the grid where he liked to sit, cross-legged on the steel girders.

Lauren's stomach gave a little flip and her heart beat harder. She felt the blood cursing through her veins, filling her with energy. She barely noticed the wooden boards of the stage digging into her ankles and knees as she waited for her cue.

Determined not to move even her eyeballs, she stared straight ahead. She could just see Nyree in her fairy doll pose on the other side of the stage. How appropriate the role was for her, Lauren thought with affectionate exasperation. She showed so little emotion or mobility. Then Julian and Helena lifted Nyree to a different spot and Lauren could no longer see her.

Lauren's solo was in the middle of the choreography, but she was so keyed up the minutes passed like seconds. She counted the last few bars of Helena's *adage* then felt the thud as Julian leaped on to the top of the box.

Out of the corner of her eye, Lauren watched her strings straighten as Julian lifted the cross bar and pretended to control her arms and legs. Lauren's part began.

She unfolded herself from the ground and started the jerky movements of a puppet. Then, on a loud chord in the music, she threw herself into the air and landed *en pointe* in a star position. As planned, the strings, loosely attached to her costume with a tiny bit of velcro, detached with the impact and a helping tug from Julien. Lauren rounded on the toy shop owner and threw herself into the passionate and electrifying rhythm of the Argentine tango that she and Katie had chosen to replace Julian's original choice of music. Together they had found a particularly fiery recording of Piazzolla's Libertango with its spicy rhythms and fiendish melody. It was the perfect mixture of classical and modern, allowing Lauren to showcase her brilliance in both genres.

Halfway through the piece, she and Julian danced together. They leaped across the stage, chasing and retreating, as they battled for supremacy in a powerful fight dance during which Lauren attached the strings to the toy shop owner and she became the puppet master.

As the accordion drove the music to the climax, Lauren leaped onto the box. And on the last beat, when the magic wore off, she took her final triumphant pose with Julian crumpled below her like the puppet she had been.

The audience burst out clapping. No one else had got a round of applause midway, and Lauren struggled to hide her smile of delight while the rest of the choreography unfolded around her.

As the curtain came down to warm applause, the dancers all scrambled for the wings. They had to vacate the stage as quickly as possible so it could be set for the last choreography by Ethan's House, Carmen.

"Nyree!" Lauren called in a loud whisper. "Come on!"

Grace floated beside Lauren as she strode over to Nyree who was still in her fairy doll pose with her back to Lauren.

Lauren grabbed her arm. Nyree gave a shudder as though she was just waking up. She turned to Lauren, her face alive with delight.

"Wow!" she breathed. "That was amazing! I loved it!"

Lauren's mouth fell open. Grace clapped her hands.

"*Isn't it wonderful, Lauren?*" she whispered. "*What the joy of ballet can do?*"

Nyree skipped to the dressing room, to the amusement of everyone around, and Lauren followed, her own face wreathed in smiles too.

The two girls changed out of their costumes and went to join the others in the auditorium. As Lauren slipped onto the seat Jay had saved for her, she spotted the turquoise hair of Piper Lapiz a few rows in front. The journalist's head was bent and Lauren could see her elbows jiggling as she tapped on her tablet.

Lauren leaned across to Alfie. "Have you told Piper you haven't got any footage?" she asked in a low voice.

Alfie shook his head. "Not yet," he whispered back. "I'll catch her at the end of the show. Well done, by the way. You were brilliant!"

Lauren grinned and jerked her thumb towards Jay and Katie. "It wouldn't have happened without them," she declared.

The lights went down and everyone settled back in their seats for the final performance of the evening by Carmen House.

Xavier Mendoza's choreography was astounding. Ethan was on fire as he executed his signature falls and spins. His daring and acrobatic skills had the audience holding their breath. The applause at the end was deafening and everyone in Lauren's row leaped to their feet, whistling and calling their admiration.

Lauren saw Katie jumping up and down, her face pink with pride, as she chanted Ethan's name along with the rest of Year Nine. The auditorium lights came up, and from the stage Ethan met Katie's gaze and gave her a surreptitious thumbs-up. Lauren's tummy did a strange swoop. What was all that about? Probably disappointment that there was no hope for Spartacus House now. She caught Katie's eye and gave her a mock salute.

While they waited for the judges to come to their decision, everyone piled into the foyer. The noise, with the entire audience discussing their opinions on each House's entry, made Lauren's head ring.

She looked round for a quiet place to escape to and saw Piper Lapiz standing alone in a corner, making frantic notes on a tablet. Peering over her shoulder, and frowning, was Rodney. Nyree was watching them, her mouth curving into a smile. Lauren looked for Grace and saw her floating towards Rodney with a worried look on her face.

At a tap on her shoulder, Lauren spun round. Alfie was standing there looking a little sheepish. "You wouldn't come with me, would you? To tell Piper that we didn't get anything?"

"Sure!" Lauren nodded, chuffed that Alfie had asked her and not Allison, who was hovering by the door to backstage. Who was she waiting for? Lauren wondered. Then she and Alfie pushed through the crowds to Piper.

Alfie cleared his throat loudly before saying, "Miss Lapiz?"

"Yes?" Piper looked up, her eyes slightly dazed, as though she were still thinking about what she was writing.

"It's me, Alfie." He held out the memory stick. "The, er, ghost hunter, remember?"

"Oh, yes. Yes. Sorry. " Piper took the stick and raised an eyebrow.

"I'm afraid I didn't get anything," Alfie admitted. "There was nothing in the cellar. Or at least, my detector didn't show anything. It doesn't mean to say there aren't ghosts at Amberwood," he added in a desperate bid to keep the dream alive, "but I'm sorry, you won't be able to do your article."

Piper looked surprised. "Are you kidding? After what I've seen this evening, I couldn't be more excited! This is far more newsworthy than some old ghosts! It's like being in the West End, Covent Garden, and Broadway all rolled into one. I had no idea Amberwood produced work of such a professional standard."

She slipped the memory stick into her pocket and snapped shut her tablet. At the same moment, the bell rang for everyone to go back to their seats, and she rushed away.

Lauren felt a rush of relief. Piper wasn't going to pursue ghosts anymore! Grace was doing a celebratory swirl, but Rodney looked as though he'd been told Christmas was cancelled forever. He swerved out of Piper's path, his face a picture of disgust.

"'Oo's she calling 'some old ghosts'," he fumed.

Lauren and Nyree laughed out loud.

"What's so funny?" Alfie asked.

"Nothing," Lauren assured him, hurriedly straightening her face. "It's just something between me and Nyree. Let's go and catch the results."

And they followed the crowd back into the auditorium.

Chapter Twenty-Three

A long table occupied the centre of the stage and the four judges, one of whom was Mrs Herriott, were sitting behind it, facing the audience.

Mrs Herriott stood and took the microphone. Instantly, the theatre fell silent. First, she introduced the other three judges, then she surveyed the auditorium and smiled.

"A correction, or piece of advice, given in an exam or performance situation, is rarely forgotten," she said. "Artists, and in fact anyone in the creative world, need to be able to take constructive criticism and use it, without feeling slighted. Consequently, this evening, we're not going to hand you the results straight away. This has been a wonderful learning experience for you and now you need to hear how you can do better next time."

People shifted in their seats and sat up expectantly.

"So, before we announce the winner," Mrs Herriott continued, "our esteemed judges are going to give you their comments on each of the choreographies. We will do them in order of appearance." She turned to the judge sitting at the right-hand end of the table. "Mr Jameson, would you like to begin with your thoughts on Sylphides House?"

The headmistress handed the microphone to a tall man with grey hair in a tight ponytail. Lauren checked her programme. He was head of a school in the south and had been a principal dancer with one of the biggest ballet companies in the world. Well, he should know his stuff!

Mr Jameson was complimentary about every piece. Lauren's hopes rose when he made special mention of the fact that Spartacus had given an old-fashioned theme a modern feel by using up-to-date toys. Then she thought she would burst with pride when another judge, heavily biased towards modern dance, complimented her by name on her performance. Katie, sitting next to her, grabbed her arm and squeezed it hard.

The judges seemed unanimous in their opinion that Lauren's solo outshone the rest of the piece both in its performance and in the choice of steps and music. They suggested that a more consistent approach to the rest of the choreography would be of great benefit, which made Lauren's cheeks turn scarlet.

They complimented Sylphides House on Hazel's pas de deux and the seamless integration of her corps de ballet, pointing out that a larger number of corps members would have made it more dramatic. Surely Amberwood had a huge pool of talent to plunder? And their only criticism of Bayadere House was the choice of costumes which they felt detracted from the choreography itself.

Lauren could hear Allison venting her disagreement to Emily and Nicola and hardly listening to the rest of the comments.

All the judges' opinions were so different, it was impossible to guess who had won. In fact, Lauren wondered how they had come to an agreement at all. Although they all seemed awed by Carmen's contribution, they were not all huge fans of modern dance.

Eventually the reviews came to an end and Mrs Herriott got to her feet again. She crossed the stage to a small podium which was displaying the House Cup. "In third place," she announced with no introduction, "is Sylphides House with 32 points."

Everyone clapped and the Year Nines high-fived Alfie. After all, it was his House even if he hadn't taken part. Lauren felt her heartbeat increasing and her stomach churning. The wait was unbearable.

"In second place," Mrs Herriott paused for effect, "Bayadere House! With 34 points"

The applause wasn't loud enough to drown Allison's groan of dismay. The people sitting around her giggled and Nyree slid Lauren a disgusted look. "She should be delighted to have come second," she whispered, "not complaining about it already."

Mrs Herriott scanned the audience, letting the tension build.

Lauren's mouth was dry and her hands clammy. Could Spartacus have actually won despite all her misgivings? She could barely breathe and thought she would suffocate if Mrs Herriott didn't get on with it.

"And it is my pleasure to reveal that first place goes to... Carmen House with their magnificent modern choreography and 37 points."

The applause exploded all round and people rose to their feet, clapping and stamping. Ethan grinned so widely that Lauren thought his face would split in two. Katie, sobbing with happiness, had thrown her arms around him and was trying to spin him round in the tiny space between seats.

Lauren punched him on the arm as he pushed past to go onstage with his House to accept the cup. She was genuinely delighted for Ethan. He deserved the success. His solo had been so amazing. But she couldn't help feeling disappointed that Spartacus House had come last.

Ethan grinned at her and squeezed her shoulder. Lauren's tummy wobbled again, and she returned his grin with a shaky smile. Then she clapped till her hands were stinging as Xavier accepted the cup on behalf of his House. He pulled Ethan to the centre of the group and held up his arm for an extra round of applause.

Eventually everyone settled down again. Carmen House returned to the auditorium for Mrs Herriott's final speech. There was a wave of laughter when she ended by introducing a new rule: "From now on," she said, her eyes raking the audience and resting momentarily on Piper's turquoise hair, "no ghost-hunting devices are permitted at the school. Students are here to study dance, not poke about in the past, unless it is studying classical ballets!"

Alfie groaned. "Now I'll never know whether my gadget works or not," he complained, while his classmates laughed.

Students, visitors and staff surged out of the auditorium to gather in the foyer and congratulate people all over again.

"*Well, I, for one, am delighted by the new rule*," Grace whispered as Lauren, Katie and Nyree watched Piper Lapiz gathering Carmen House together to take photos for the newspaper.

Jay and Alfie stood nearby, with Mark on the fringes. It was the nearest he'd got to Lauren and Katie all day. Lauren caught his eye and tilted her head to show there were no hard feelings. He flushed and replied with a slight nod.

When the photo shoot was over, Ethan joined the group and threw his arm round Katie's shoulders.

Grace and Rodney were still floating beside Lauren and Nyree. *"Do you mind that your House didn't win?"* Grace whispered as they watched.

"I think you should've," Rodney declared. *"Though fourth is a pretty good place too."*

"Not when it's fourth out of four!" Lauren whispered, pretending she was talking to Nyree and trying to sound light-hearted.

"It don't matter. You were the absolute tops, Miss Lauren! All the judges said so. And you weren't so bad yourself, Miss Nyree!"

Nyree rewarded him with a rare smile.

Lauren cast a glance towards Ethan, with Katie hanging on his arm. "I guess you can't win 'em all," she murmured.

Then Jay's voice broke her out of her reverie. "Miss Lapiz," he called to Piper who was nearly at the door. "Did you enjoy the show?"

The journalist spun round, her eyes sparkling, and Lauren, Nyree and the ghosts collapsed into laughter as she said, "Enjoy it? It was truly haunting!"

The End

OTHER BOOKS BY ELEANOR DIXON

In the Amberwood Hall Series:

*The Ghosts of Amberwood (Prequel. Ebook only)
The Graceful Ghost
Ballet School Boys

**You can download a free copy of THE GHOSTS OF AMBERWOOD by joining Eleanor's mailing list. Details follow.*

Tally and the Angel Book One, India
Tally and the Angel Book Two, Canada
and coming soon,
Tally and the Angel Book Three, Japan

DON'T KEEP ME A SECRET!

Have you enjoyed BALLET SCHOOL RUMOURS?
If so, please write a review! Authors love to hear from their readers.
It takes a long time to write a book and there's nothing better than hearing from readers who have liked it. Not only that, it helps other readers, children, parents and grandparents find the story.
You can let Eleanor Dixon know how much you enjoyed BALLET SCHOOL RUMOURS by leaving a short review on Amazon, Goodreads, or your preferred online store. If you're under age 13, ask a grown up to help you.
AND DON'T FORGET – be sure not to give away any of the story's secrets!

JOIN ELEANOR'S MAILING LIST OR FOLLOW HER ON SOCIAL MEDIA

You can be the first to learn about new books or special offers by joining Eleanor's mailing list.
Go to: www.eleanordixon.com
And receive a Free Copy of The Ghosts of Amberwood

Follow Eleanor on:

Instagram: theburrowinthefield

Facebook: Eleanor Dixon@theburreau

ACKNOWLEDGEMENTS

There is always someone to thank in the creation of a book. It couldn't happen without a good editorial team, and I have the best! You know who you are.

A huge thank you goes this time to David Needham, Squadron Leader (Retired) for all his advice on aviation and the RAF.

And, as ever, my humble gratitude to my wonderful husband, Shaun, and my three muses, Digit (dog), Moji (cat) and Mokey (Dog)

Printed in Great Britain
by Amazon

22413326R00098